D0428999

Batting
Against Castro

Batting Against Castro

STORIES BY

Jim Shepard

Alfred A. Knopf
New York
1996

THIS IS A BORZOI BOOK
PUBLISHED BY ALFRED A. KNOPF, INC.

http://www.randomhouse.com

Stories from this collection were originally published in the following: *The Atlantic Monthly,* "Atomic Tourism" and "Eustace"; *Epoch,* "The Touch of the Dead"; *Esquire,* "Ida"; *GQ,* "Messiah"; *Harper's,* "Runway"; *The New Yorker,* "Reach for the Sky"; *The Paris Review,* "Batting Against Castro"; *Southwest Review,* "Who We Are, What We're Doing"; *TriQuarterly,* "Nosferatu."

Library of Congress Cataloging-in-Publication Data
Shepard, Jim.
Batting against Castro : stories / by Jim Shepard.
—1st ed.
p.   cm.
ISBN 0-679-44668-0 (alk. paper)
1. Manners and customs—Fiction.   I. Title.
PS3569.H39384B38   1996
813'.54—dc20   95-49316
                CIP   .

Manufactured in the United States of America
First Edition

For Stephen Minot, John Hawkes, and John Gardner

Contents

Strangers

Batting
Against Castro

In 1951 you couldn't get us to talk politics. Ballplayers then would just as soon talk bed-wetting as talk politics. Tweener Jordan brought up the H-bomb one seventh inning, sitting there tarring up his useless Louisville Slugger at the end of a Bataan Death March of a road trip when it was one hundred and four on the field and about nine of us in a row had just been tied in knots by Maglie and it looked like we weren't going to get anyone on base in the next five weeks except for those hit by pitches, at which point someone down the end of the bench told Tweener to put a lid on it, and he did, and that was the end of the H-bomb as far as the Philadelphia Phillies were concerned.

I was one or two frosties shy of outweighing my bat and wasn't exactly known as Mr. Heavy Hitter; in fact me and Charley Caddell, another Pinemaster from the Phabulous Phillies, were known far and wide as such banjo hitters that they called us—right to our faces, right during a game, like confidence or bucking up a

3

teammate was for noolies and nosedroops—Flatt and Scruggs. Pick us a tune, boys, they'd say, our own teammates, when it came time for the eighth and ninth spots in the order to save the day. And Charley and I would grab our lumber and shoot each other looks like we were the Splinter himself, misunderstood by everybody, and up we'd go to the plate against your basic New-combe or Erskine cannon volleys. Less knowledgeable fans would cheer. The organist would pump through the motions and the twenty-seven thousand who did show up (PHILS WHACKED IN TWI-NIGHTER; SLUMP CONTINUES; LOCALS SEEK TO SALVAGE LAST GAME OF HOME STAND) wouldn't say boo. Our runners aboard would stand there like they were watching furniture movers. One guy in our dugout would clap. A pigeon would set down in right field and gook around. Newcombe or Erskine would look in at us like litter was blowing across their line of sight. They'd paint the corners with a few unhittable ones just to let us know what a mis-match this was. Then Charley would dink one to second. It wouldn't make a sound in the glove. I'd strike out. And the fans would cuff their kids or scratch their rears and cheer. It was like they were celebrating just how bad we could be.

I'd always come off the field looking at my bat, trademark up, like I couldn't figure out what happened. You'd think by that point I would've. I tended to be hitting about .143.

Whenever we were way down, in the 12-to-2 range, Charley played them up, our sixth- or seventh- or, worse, ninth-inning Waterloos—tipped his cap and did some minor posing—and for his trouble got showered with whatever the box seats didn't feel like finishing: peanuts, beer, the occasional hot-dog bun. On what was the last straw before this whole Cuba thing, after we'd gone down one-two and killed a bases-loaded rally for the second time that day, the boxes around the dugout got so bad that Charley went back out and took a curtain call, like he'd clubbed a round-tripper. The fans howled for parts of his body. The Dodgers across the way laughed and pointed. In the time it took Charley to lift his cap and wave someone caught him in the mouth with a metal whistle from a Cracker Jack box and chipped a tooth.

"You stay on the pine," Skip said to him while he sat there trying to wiggle the ivory in question. "I'm tired of your antics." Skip was our third-year manager who'd been through it all, seen it all, and lost most of the games along the way.

"What's the hoo-ha?" Charley wanted to know. "We're down eleven–nothing."

Skip said that Charley reminded him of Dummy Hoy, the deaf-mute who played for Cincinnati all those years ago. Skip was always saying things like that. The first time he saw me shagging flies he said I was the picture of Skeeter Scalzi.

"Dummy Hoy batted .287 lifetime," Charley said. "I'll take that anytime."

The thing was, we were both good glove men. And this was the Phillies. If you could do anything right, you were worth at least a spot on the pine. After Robin Roberts, our big gun on the mound, it was Katie bar the door.

"We're twenty-three games back," Skip said. "This isn't the time for bush-league stunts."

It was late in the season, and Charley was still holding that tooth and in no mood for a gospel from Skip. He let fly with something in the abusive range, and I'm ashamed to say that I became a disruptive influence on the bench and backed him up.

Quicker than you could say Wally Pipp, we were on our way to Allentown for some Double A discipline.

Our ride out there was not what you'd call high-spirited. The Allentown bus ground gears and did ten, tops. It really worked over those switchbacks on the hills, to maximize the dust coming through the windows. Or you could shut the windows and bake muffins.

Charley was across the aisle, sorting through the paper. He'd looked homicidal from the bus station on.

"We work on our hitting, he's got to bring us back," I said. "Who else has he got?" Philadelphia's major-league franchise was at that point in pretty bad shape, with a lot of kids filling gaps left by the hospital patients.

Charley mentioned an activity involving Skip's mother. It colored the ears of the woman sitting in front of us.

It was then I suggested the winter leagues, Mexico or Cuba.

"How about Guam?" Charley said. "How about the Yukon?" He hawked out the window.

Here was my thinking: The season was almost over in Allentown, which was also, by the way, in the cellar. We probably weren't going back up afterwards. That meant that starting October we either cooled our heels playing pepper in Pennsylvania, or we played winter ball. I was for Door Number Two.

Charley and me, we had to do something about our self-esteem. It got so I'd wince just to see my name in the sports pages—before I knew what it was about, just to see my name. Charley's full name was Charles Owen Caddell, and he carried a handsome suitcase around the National League that had his initials, C.O.C., in big letters near the handle. When asked what they stood for, he always said, "Can o' Corn."

Skip we didn't go to for fatherly support. Skip tended to be hard on the nonregulars, who he referred to as "you egg-sucking noodle-hanging gutter trash."

Older ballplayers talked about what it was like to lose it: the way your teammates would start giving you the look, the way you could see in their eyes, Three years ago he'd make that play, or He's lost a step going to the hole; the quickness isn't there. The difference was, Charley and me, we'd seen that look since we were twelve.

So Cuba seemed like the savvy move: a little seasoning, a little time in the sun, some senoritas, drinks with hats, maybe a curveball Charley *could* hit, a heater I could do more than foul off.

Charley took some convincing. He'd sit there in the Allentown dugout, riding the pine even in Allentown, whistling air through his chipped tooth and making faces at me. This Cuba thing was stupid, he'd say. He knew a guy played for the Athletics went down to Mexico or someplace, drank a cup of water with bugs in it that would've turned Dr. Salk's face white, and went belly-up between games of a doubleheader. "Shipped home in a box they had to *seal*," Charley said. He'd tell that story, and his tooth would whistle for emphasis.

But really what other choice did we have? Between us we had the money to get down there, and I knew a guy on the Pirates who was able to swing the connections. I finished the year batting .143 in the bigs and .167 in Allentown. Charley hit his weight and pulled off three errors in an inning his last game. When we left, our Allentown manager said, "Boys, I hope you hit the bigs again. Because we sure can't use you around here."

So down we went on the train and then the slow boat, accompanied the whole way by a catcher from the Yankees' system, a big bird from Minnesota named Ericksson. Ericksson was out of Triple A and apparently had a fan club there because he was so fat. I guess it had gotten so he couldn't field bunts. He said the Yankee brass was paying for this. They thought of it as a fat farm.

"The thing is, I'm not fat," he said. We were pulling out of some skeeter-and-water stop in central Florida. One guy sat on the train platform with his chin on his chest, asleep or dead. "That's the thing. What I am is big boned." He held up an arm and squeezed it the way you'd test a melon.

"I like having you in the window seat," Charley said, his Allentown hat down over his eyes. "Makes the whole trip shady."

Ericksson went on to talk about feet. This shortened the feel of the trip considerably. Ericksson speculated that the smallest feet in the history of the major leagues belonged to Art Herring, who wore a size three. Myril Hoag, apparently, wore one size four and one size four and a half.

We'd signed a deal with the Cienfuegos club: seven hundred a month and two-fifty for expenses. We also got a place on the beach, supposedly, and a woman to do the cleaning, though we had to pay her bus fare back and forth. It sounded a lot better than the Mexican League, which had teams with names like Coatzacoalcos. Forget the Mexican League, Charley'd said when I brought it up. Once I guess he'd heard some retreads from that circuit talking about the Scorpions, and he'd said, "They have a team with that name?" and they'd said no.

When Ericksson finished with feet he wanted to talk politics. Not only the whole Korean thing—truce negotiations, we're on a thirty-one-hour train ride with someone who wants to talk truce negotiations—but this whole thing with Cuba and other Latin American countries and Kremlin expansionism. Ericksson could get going on Kremlin expansionism.

"Charley's not much on politics," I said, trying to turn off the spigot.

"You can talk politics if you want," Charley said from under his hat. "Talk politics. I got a degree. I can keep up. I got a B.S. from Schenectady." The B.S. stood for "Boots and Shoes," meaning he worked in a factory.

So there we were in Cuba. Standing on the dock, peering into the sun, dragging our big duffel bags like dogs that wouldn't co-operate.

We're standing there sweating on our bags and wondering

where the team rep who's supposed to meet us is, and meanwhile a riot breaks out a block and a half away. We thought it was a block party at first. This skinny guy in a pleated white shirt and one of those cigar-ad pointed beards was racketing away at the crowd, which was yelling and carrying on. He was over six feet. He looked strong, wiry, but in terms of heft somewhere between flyweight and poster child. He was scoring big with some points he was making holding up a bolt of cloth. He said something that got them all going, and up he went onto their shoulders, and they paraded him around past the storefronts, everybody shouting "*Castro! Castro! Castro!*" which Charley and me figured was the guy's name. We were still sitting there in the sun like idiots. They circled around past us and stopped. They got quiet, and we looked at each other. The man of the hour was giving us his fearsome bandido look. He was tall. He was skinny. He was just a kid. He didn't look at all happy to see us.

He looked about ready to say something that was not a welcome when the *policia* waded in, swinging clubs like they were getting paid by the concussion. Which is when the riot started. The team rep showed up. We got hustled out of there.

We'd arrived, it turned out, a few weeks into the season. Cienfuegos was a game down in the loss column to its big rival, Marianao. Charley called it Marianne.

Cuba took more than a little getting used to. There was the heat: one team we played had a stadium that sat in a kind of natural bowl that held in the sun and dust. The dust floated around you like a golden fog. It glittered. Water streamed down your face and back. Your glove dripped. One of our guys had trouble finding the plate, and while I stood there creeping in on the infield dirt, sweat actually puddled around my feet.

There were the fans: one night they pelted each other and the field with live snakes. They sang, endlessly. Every team in the

Liga de Baseball Cubana had its own slogan, to be chanted during rallies, during seventh-inning stretches, or just when the crowd felt bored. The Elefantes' was *"El paso del elefante es lento pero aplastante."* Neither of us knew Spanish, and by game two we knew our slogan by heart.

"What *is* that?" Charley finally asked Ericksson, who *habla*'d okay. "What are they saying?"

"'The Elephant passes slowly,'" Ericksson said, "'but it squashes.'"

There were the pranks: as the outsiders, Charley and me expected the standards—the shaving-cream-in-the-shoe, the multiple hotfoot—but even so never got tired of the bird-spider-in-the-cap, or the crushed-chilies-in-the-water-fountain. Many's the time, after such good-natured ribbing from our Latino teammates, we'd still be holding our ribs, toying with our bats, and wishing we could identify the particular jokester in question.

There was the travel: the bus trips to the other side of the island that seemed to take short careers. I figured Cuba, when I figured it at all, to be about the size of Long Island, but I was not close. During one of those trips Ericksson, the only guy still in a good mood, leaned over his seat back and gave me the bad news: if you laid Cuba over the eastern United States, he said, it'd stretch from New York to Chicago. Or something like that.

And from New York to Chicago the neighborhood would go right down the toilet, Charley said, next to me.

Sometimes we'd leave right after a game, I mean without showering, and that meant no matter how many open windows you were able to manage you smelled bad feet and armpit all the way back. On the mountain roads and switchbacks we counted roadside crosses and smashed guardrails on the hairpin turns.

One time Charley, his head out the window to get any kind of air, looked way down into an arroyo and kept looking. I asked him what he could see down there. He said a glove and some bats.

And finally there was what Ericksson called a Real Lack of Perspective. He was talking, of course, about that famous South of the Border hotheadedness we'd all seen even in the bigs. In our first series against Marianao after Charley and I joined the team (the two of us went two for twenty-six, and we got swept; so much for gringos to the rescue), an argument at home plate—not about whether the guy was out, but about whether the tag had been too hard—brought out both managers, both benches, a blind batboy who felt around everyone's legs for the discarded lumber, a drunk who'd been sleeping under the stands, reporters, a photographer, a would-be beauty queen, the radio announcers, and a large number of interested spectators. I forget how it came out.

After we dropped a doubleheader in Havana our manager had a pot broken over his head. The pot held a plant, which he kept and replanted. After a win at home our starting third baseman was shot in the foot. We asked our manager, mostly through sign language, why. He said he didn't know why they picked the foot.

But it was more than that, too: On days off we'd sit in our hammocks and look out our floor-to-ceiling windows and our screened patios and smell our garden with its flowers with the colors from Mars and the breeze with the sea in it. We'd feel like DiMaggio in his penthouse, as big league as big league could get. We'd fish on the coral reefs for yellowtail and mackerel, for shrimp and rock lobster. We'd cook it ourselves. Ericksson started eating over, and he did great things with coconut and lime and beer.

And our hitting began to improve.

One for five, one for four, two for five, two for five with two doubles: the box scores were looking up and up, Spanish or not. One night we went to an American restaurant in Havana, and on the place on the check for comments I wrote, *I went 3 for 5 today.*

Cienfuegos went on a little streak: nine wins in a row, fourteen out of fifteen. We caught and passed Marianao. Even Ericksson was slimming down. He pounced on bunts and stomped around home plate like a man killing bees before gunning runners out. We were on a winner.

Which is why politics, like it always does, had to stick its nose in. The president of our tropical paradise, who reminded Charley more of Akim Tamiroff than Harry Truman, was a guy named Batista who was not well liked. This we could tell because when we said his name our teammates would repeat it and then spit on the ground or our feet. We decided to go easy on the political side of things and keep mum on the subject of our opinions, which we mostly didn't have. Ericksson threatened periodically to get us all into trouble or, worse, a discussion, except his Spanish didn't always hold up, and the first time he tried to talk politics everyone agreed with what he was saying and then brought him a bedpan.

Neither of us, as I said before, was much for the front of the newspaper, but you didn't have to be Mr. News to see that Cuba was about as bad as it got in terms of who was running what: the payoffs got to the point where we figured that guys getting sworn in for public office put their hands out instead of up. We paid off local mailmen to get our mail. We paid off traffic cops to get through intersections. It didn't seem like the kind of thing that could go on forever, especially since most of the Cubans on the island didn't get expense money.

So this Batista—"Akim" to Charley—wasn't doing a good job, and it looked like your run-of-the-mill Cuban was hot about that. He kept most of the money for himself and his pals. If you were on the outs and needed food or medicine it was your hard luck. And according to some of our teammates, when you went to jail—for whatever, for spitting on the sidewalk—bad things happened to you. Relatives wrote you off.

So there were a lot of protests, *demonstraciones*, that winter, and driving around town in cabs we always seemed to run into them, which meant trips out to eat or to pick up the paper might run half the day. It was the only nonfinable excuse for showing up late to the ballpark.

But then the demonstrations started at the games, in the stands. And guess who'd usually be leading them, in his little pleated shirt and orange-and-black Marianao cap? We'd be two or three innings in, and the crowd out along the third-base line would get up like the chorus in a Busby Berkeley musical and start singing and swaying back and forth, their arms in the air. They were not singing the team slogan. The first time it happened Batista himself was in the stands, surrounded by like forty bodyguards. He had his arms crossed and was staring over at Castro, who had *his* arms crossed and was staring back. Charley was at the plate, and I was on deck.

Charley walked over to me, bat still on his shoulder. I'm not sure anybody had called time. The pitcher was watching the crowd, too. "Now what is this?" Charley wanted to know.

I told him it could have been a religious thing, or somebody's birthday. He looked at me. "I mean like a national hero's, or something," I said.

He was still peering over at Castro's side of the crowd, swinging his bat to keep limber, experimenting with that chipped-tooth whistle. "What're they saying?" he asked.

"It's in Spanish," I said.

Charley shook his head and then shot a look over to Batista on the first-base side. "Akim's gonna love this," he said. But Batista sat there like this happened all the time. The umpire straightened every inch of clothing behind his chest protector and then had enough and started signaling play to resume, so Charley got back into the batter's box, dug in, set himself, and unloaded big time on the next pitch and put it on a line without meaning to into the crowd on the third-base side. A whole side of the stands ducked, and a couple of people flailed and went down like they were shot. You could see people standing over them.

Castro in the meantime stood in the middle of this with his arms still folded, like Peary at the Pole, or Admiral Whoever taking grapeshot across the bow. You had to give him credit.

Charley stepped out of the box and surveyed the damage, cringing a little. Behind him I could see Batista, his hands together over his head, shaking them in congratulation.

"Wouldn't you know it," Charley said, still a little rueful. "I finally get a hold of one and zing it foul."

"I hope nobody's dead over there," I said. I could see somebody holding up a hat and looking down, like that was all that was left. Castro was still staring out over the field.

"Wouldn't that be our luck," Charley said, but he did look worried.

Charley ended up doubling, which the third-base side booed, and then stealing third, which they booed even more. While he stood on the bag brushing himself off and feeling quite the pepperpot, Castro stood up and caught him flush on the back of the head with what looked like an entire burrito of some sort. Mashed beans flew.

The crowd loved it. Castro sat back down, accepting congratulations all around. Charley, when he recovered, made a move like he was going into the stands, but no one in the stadium went for the bluff. So he just stood there with his hands on his hips, the splattered third baseman pointing him out to the crowd and laughing. He stood there on third and waited for me to bring him home so he could spike the catcher to death. He had onions and probably some ground meat on his cap.

That particular Cold War crisis ended with my lining out, a rocket, to short.

In the dugout afterwards I told Charley it had been that same guy, Castro, from our first day on the dock. He said that that figured and that he wanted to work on his bat control so he could kill the guy with a line drive if he ever saw him in the stands again.

This Castro came up a lot. There was a guy on the team, a light-hitting left fielder named Rafa, who used to lecture us in Spanish, very worked up. Big supporter of Castro. You could see he was upset about something. Ericksson and I would nod, like we'd given what he was on about some serious thought, and were just about to weigh in on that very subject. I'd usually end the meetings by giving him a thumbs-up and heading out onto the field. Ericksson knew it was about politics so he was interested. Charley had no patience for it on good days and hearing this guy bring up Castro didn't help. Every so often he'd call across our lockers, "He wants to know if you want to meet his sister."

Finally Rafa took to bringing an interpreter, and he'd find us at dinners, waiting for buses, taking warm-ups, and up would come the two of them, Rafa and his interpreter, like this was sports day at the U.N. Rafa would rattle on while we went about our business, and then his interpreter would take over. His interpreter said things like, "This is not your tropical playground." He said things like, "The government of the United States will come to understand the Cuban people's right to self-determination." He said things like, "The people will rise up and crush the octopus of the north."

"He means the Yankees, Ericksson," Charley said.

Ericksson meanwhile had that big Nordic brow all furrowed, ready to talk politics.

You could see Rafa thought he was getting through. He went off on a real rip, and when he finished the interpreter said only, "The poverty of the people in our Cuba is very bad."

Ericksson hunkered down and said, "And the people think Batista's the problem?"

"Lack of money's the problem," Charley said. The interpreter gave him the kind of look the hotel porter gives you when you show up with seventeen bags. Charley made a face back at him as if to say, Am I right or wrong?

"The poverty of the people is very bad," the interpreter said again. He was stubborn. He didn't have to tell us: on one road trip we saw a town, like a used-car lot, of whole families, big families, living in abandoned cars. Somebody had a cradle thing worked out for a baby in an overturned fender.

"What do you want from us?" Charley asked.

"You are supporting the corrupt system," the interpreter said. Rafa hadn't spoken and started talking excitedly, probably asking what'd just been said.

Charley took some cuts and snorted. "Guy's probably been changing everything Rafa wanted to say," he said.

We started joking that poor Rafa'd only been trying to talk about how to hit a curve. They both gave up on us, and walked off. Ericksson followed them.

"Dag Hammarskjöld," Charley said, watching him go. When he saw my face he said, "I read the papers."

But this Castro guy set the tone for the other ballparks. The demonstrations continued more or less the same way (without the burrito) for the last two weeks of the season, and with three games left we found ourselves with a two-game lead on Marianao, and we finished the season guess where against guess who.

This was a big deal to the fans because Marianao had no imports, no Americans, on their team. Even though they had about seven guys with big-league talent, to the Cubans this was David and Goliath stuff. Big America vs. Little Cuba, and our poor Rafa found himself playing for Big America.

So we lost the first two games, by ridiculous scores, scores like 18–5 and 16–1. The kind of scores where you're playing out the string after the third inning. Marianao was charged up and we weren't. Most of the Cuban guys on our team, as you'd figure, were a little confused. They were all trying—money was involved here—but the focus wasn't exactly there. In the first game we came unraveled after Rafa dropped a pop-up that went seven thousand feet up into the sun, and in the second we were just wiped out by a fat forty-five-year-old pitcher that people said when he had his control and some sleep the night before was unbeatable.

Castro and Batista were at both games. During the seventh-inning stretch of the second game, with Marianao now tied for first place, Castro led the third-base side in a Spanish version of "Take Me Out to the Ball Game."

They jeered us—Ericksson, Charley and me—every time we came up. And the more we let it get to us, the worse we did. Ericksson was pressing, I was pressing, Charley was pressing. So we let each other down. But what made it worse was with every roar after one of our strikeouts, with every stadium-shaking celebration after a ball went through our legs, we felt like we were letting America down, like some poor guy on an infantry charge who can't even hold up the flag, dragging it along the ground. It got to us.

When Charley was up, I could hear him talking to himself: "The kid can still hit. Ball was in on him, but he got that bat head out in front."

When I was up, I could hear the chatter from Charley: "Gotta have this one. This is where we need you, big guy."

On Friday Charley made the last out. On Saturday I did. On Saturday night we went to the local bar that seemed the safest and got paralyzed. Ericksson stayed home, resting up for the rubber match.

Our Cuban skipper had a clubhouse meeting before the last game. It was hard to have a clear-the-air meeting when some of the teammates didn't understand the language, and were half paralyzed with hangovers besides, but they went on with it anyway, pointing at us every so often. I got the feeling the suggestion was that the Americans be benched for the sake of morale.

To our Cuban skipper's credit, and because he was more contrary than anything else, he penciled us in.

Just to stick it in Marianao's ear, he penciled us into the 1-2-3 spots in the order.

The game started around three in the afternoon. It was one of the worst hangovers I'd ever had. I walked out into the Cuban sun, the first to carry the hopes of Cienfuegos and America to the plate, and decided that as a punishment I'd been struck blind. The crowd chanted, "The Elephant passes slowly, but it squashes." I struck out, though I have only the umpire's say-so on that.

Charley struck out too. Back on the bench he squinted like someone looking into car headlights. "It was a good pitch," he said. "I mean it sounded like a good pitch. I didn't see it."

But Ericksson, champion of clean living, stroked one out. It put the lid on some of the celebrating in the stands. We were a little too hungover to go real crazy when he got back to the dugout, but I think he understood.

Everybody, in fact, was hitting but us. A couple guys behind Ericksson including Rafa put together some doubles, and we had a 3–0 lead which stood up all the way to the bottom of the inning, when Marianao batted around and through its lineup and our starter and went into the top of the second leading 6–3.

Our guys kept hitting, and so did their guys. At the end of seven we'd gone through four pitchers and Marianao five, Charley and I were regaining use of our limbs, and the score was Cuba 11, Land of the Free 9. We got another run on a passed ball. In the ninth we came up one run down with the sun setting in our eyes over the center-field fence and yours truly leading off. The crowd was howling like something I'd never heard before. Castro had everybody up on the third-base side and pointing at me. Their arms moved together like they were working some kind of hex. Marianao's pitcher—by now the sixth—was the forty-five-year-old fat guy who'd worked the day before. The bags under his eyes were bigger than mine. He snapped off three nasty curves, and I beat one into the ground and ran down the first-base line with the jeering following me the whole way.

He broke one off on Charley, too, and Charley grounded to first. The noise was solid, a wall. Everyone was waving Cuban flags.

I leaned close to Charley's ear in the dugout. "You gotta lay off those," I said.

"I never noticed anything wrong with my ability to pull the ball on an outside pitch," he said.

"Then you're the only one in Cuba who hasn't," I said.

But in the middle of this local party with two strikes on him Ericsson hit his second dinger, probably the first time he'd had two in a game since Pony League. He took his time on his home-run trot, all slimmed-down two hundred sixty pounds of him, and at the end he did a somersault and landed on home plate with both feet.

For the Marianao crowd it was like the Marines had landed. When the ball left his bat the crowd noise got higher and higher

pitched and then just stopped and strangled. You could hear Ericksson breathing hard as he came back to the bench. You could
hear the pop of the umpire's new ball in the pitcher's glove.

"The Elephant passes slowly, but it squashes," Charley sang,
from his end of the bench.

That sent us into extra innings, a lot of extra innings. It got
dark. Nobody scored. Charley struck out with the bases loaded in
the sixteenth, and when he came back to the bench someone
had poured beer on the dugout roof and it was dripping through
onto his head. He sat there under it. He said, "I deserve it," and I
said, "Yes, you do."

The Marianao skipper overmanaged and ran out of pitchers.
He had an outfielder come in and fling a few, and the poor guy
walked our eighth and ninth hitters with pitches in the dirt, off
the backstop, into the seats. I was up. There was a conference on
the mound that included some fans and a vendor. Then there
was a roar, and I followed everyone's eyes and saw Castro up and
moving through the seats to the field. Someone threw him a
glove.

He crossed to the mound, and the Marianao skipper watched
him come and then handed him the ball when he got there like
his relief ace had just come in from the pen. Castro took the outfielder's hat for himself, but that was about it for a uniform. The
tails of his pleated shirt hung out. His pants looked like Rudolph
Valentino's. He was wearing dress shoes.

I turned to the ump. "Is this an exhibition at this point?" I said.
He said something in Spanish that I assumed was "You're in a
world of trouble now."

The crowd, which had screamed itself out hours ago, got its
second wind. Hurricanes, dust devils, sandstorms in the Sa-
hara—I don't know what the sound was like. When you opened
your mouth it came and took your words away.

I looked over at Batista, who was sitting on his hands. How long was this guy going to last if he couldn't even police the national pastime?

Castro toed the rubber, worked the ball in his hand, and stared at me like he hated everyone I'd ever been associated with. He was right-handed. He fussed with his cap. He had a windmill delivery. I figured, Let him have his fun, and he wound up and cut loose with a fastball behind my head.

The crowd reacted like he'd struck me out. I got out of the dirt and did the pro brush-off, taking time with all parts of my uniform. Then I stood in again, and he broke a pretty fair curve in by my knees, and down I went again.

What was I supposed to do? Take one for the team? Take one for the country? Get a hit, and never leave the stadium alive? He came back with his fastball high, and I thought, Enough of this, and tomahawked it foul. We glared at each other. He came back with a change-up—had this guy pitched somewhere, for somebody?—again way inside, and I thought, Forget it, and took it on the hip. The umpire waved me to first, and the crowd screamed about it like we were cheating.

I stood on first. The bases were now loaded for Charley. You could see the Marianao skipper wanted Castro off the mound, but what could he do?

Charley steps to the plate, and it's like the fans had been holding back on the real noisemaking up to this point. There are trumpets, cowbells, police whistles, sirens, and the godawful noise of someone by the foul pole banging two frying pans together. The attention seems to unnerve Charley. I'm trying to give him the old thumbs-up from first, but he's locked in on Castro, frozen in his stance. The end of his bat's making little circles in the air. Castro gave it the old windmill and whipped a curve past his chin. Charley bailed out and stood in again. The next pitch was a curve, too, which fooled him completely. He'd been waiting on the fastball. He started to swing, realized it was a curve breaking in on him, and ducked away to save his life. The ball hit his bat anyway. It dribbled out toward Castro. Charley gaped at it and then took off for first. I took off for second. The crowd shrieked. Ten thousand people, one shriek. All Castro had to do was gun it to first and they were out of the inning. He threw it into right field.

Pandemonium. Our eighth and ninth hitters scored. The ball skipped away from the right fielder. I kept running. The catcher'd gone down to first to back up the throw. I rounded third like Man o' War, Charley not far behind me, the fans spilling out onto the field and coming at us like a wave we were beating to shore. One kid's face was a flash of spite under a Yankee hat, a woman with long scars on her neck was grabbing for my arm. And there was Castro blocking the plate, dress shoes wide apart, Valentino pants crouched and ready, his face scared and full of hate like I was the entire North American continent bearing down on him.

Reach for the Sky

Guy comes into the shelter this last Thursday, a kid, really, maybe doing it for his dad, with a female golden/Labrador cross, two or three years old. He's embarrassed, not ready for forms and questions, but we get dogs like this all the time, and I'm not letting him off the hook, not letting him out of here before I know he knows that we have to kill a lot of these dogs, dogs like his. Her name is Rita, and he says, "Rita, sit!" like being here is part of her ongoing training. Rita sits halfway and then stands again, and looks at him in that tuned-in way goldens have.

"So . . ." The kid looks at the forms I've got on the counter, like no one told him this was part of the deal. He looks at the sampler that the sister of the regional boss did for our office: A MAN KNOWS ONLY AS MUCH AS HE'S SUFFERED. ST. FRANCIS OF ASSISI. He has no answers whatsoever for the form. She's two, he thinks. Housebroken. Some shots. His dad handled all that stuff. She's spayed. Reason for surrender: she plays too rough.

She smashed this huge lamp, the kid says. Of one of those mariners with the pipe and the yellow bad-weather outfit. His dad made it in a ceramics class.

Rita looks over at me with bright interest. The kids adds, "And she's got this thing with her back legs, she limps pretty bad. The vet said she wouldn't get any better."

"What vet?" I ask. I'm not supposed to push too hard, it's no better if they abandon them on highways, but we get sixty dogs a day here, and if I can talk any of them back into their houses, great. "The vet couldn't do anything?"

"We don't have the money," the kid says.

I ask to see Rita's limp. The kid's vague, and Rita refuses to demonstrate. Her tail thumps the floor twice.

I explain the bottom of the form to the kid: when he signs it, he's giving us permission to have the dog put down if it comes to that. "She's a good dog," he says helpfully. "She'll probably get someone to like her."

So I do the animal shelter Joe Friday, which never works: "Maybe. But we get ten goldens per week. And everybody wants puppies."

"Okay, well, good luck," the kid says. He signs something on the line that looks like *Fleen*. Rita looks at him. He takes the leash, wrapping it around his forearm. At the door he says, "You be a good girl, now." Rita pants a little with a neutral expression, processing the information.

It used to be you would get owners all the time who were teary and broken up: they needed to know their dog was going to get a good home, you had to guarantee it, they needed to make their problem yours, so that they could say: Hey, when *I* left the dog, it was fine.

Their dog would always make a great pet for somebody, their

dog was always great with kids, their dog always needed A Good Home and Plenty of Room to Run. Their dog, they were pretty sure, would always be the one we'd have no trouble placing in a nice family. And when they got to the part about signing the release form for euthanasia, only once did someone, a little girl, suggest that if it came to that, they should be called back, and they'd retrieve the dog. Her mother had asked me if I had any ideas, and the girl suggested that. Her mother said, I asked *him* if *he* had any ideas.

Now you get kids: the parents don't even bring the dogs in. Behind the kid with the golden/Lab mix there's a girl who's maybe seventeen or eighteen. Benetton top, Benetton skirt, straw-blond hair, tennis tan, and a Doberman puppy. Bizarre dog for a girl like that. Chews everything, she says. She holds the puppy like a baby. As if to cooperate, the dog twists and squirms around in her arms trying to get at the pen holder to show what it can do.

Puppies chew things, I tell her, and she rolls her eyes like she knows *that*. I tell her how many dogs come in every day. I lie. I say, We've had four Doberman puppies for weeks now. She says, "There're forms or something or I just leave him?" She slides him on his back gently across the counter. His paws are in the air and he looks a little bewildered.

"If I showed you how to make him stop chewing things, would you take him back?" I ask her. The Doberman has sprawled around and gotten to his feet, taller now than we are, nails clicking tentatively on the counter.

"No," she says. She signs the form, annoyed by a sweep of hair that keeps falling forward. "We're moving anyhow." She pats the dog on the muzzle as a goodbye and he nips at her, his feet slipping and sliding like a skater's. "God," she says. She's mad at me now, too, the way people get mad at those pictures that come in the mail of cats and dogs looking at you with their noses through the chain-link fences: *Help Skipper, who lived on leather for three weeks.*

When I come back from taking the Doberman downstairs there's a middle-aged guy at the counter in a wheelchair. An Irish setter circles back and forth around the chair, winding and unwinding the black nylon leash across the guy's chest. Somebody's put some time into grooming this dog, and when the sun hits that red coat just right he looks like a million dollars.

I'm not used to wheelchair people. The guy says, "I gotta get rid of the dog."

What do you say to a guy like that? Can't you take care of him? Too much trouble? The setter's got to be eight years old.

"Is he healthy?" I ask.

"She," he says. "She's in good shape."

"Landlord problem?" I say. The guy says nothing.

"What's her name?" I ask.

"We gotta have a discussion?" the guy says. I think, This is what wheelchair people are like. The setter whines and stands her front paws on the arm of the guy's chair.

"We got forms," I say. I put them on the counter, not so close that he doesn't have to reach. He starts to sit up higher and then leans back. "What's it say?" he says.

"Sex," I say.

"Female," he says.

Breed. Irish setter. Age, eleven.

Eleven! I can feel this dog on the back of my neck. On my forehead. I can just see myself selling this eleven-year-old dog to the families that come in looking. And how long has she been with him?

I walk back and forth behind the counter, hoist myself up, flex my legs.

The guy goes, like he hasn't noticed any of that, "She does tricks."

"Tricks?" I say.

"Ellie," he says. He mimes a gun with his forefinger and thumb and points it at her. "Ellie. Reach for the sky."

Ellie is all attention. Ellie sits, and then rears up, lifting her front paws as high as a dog can lift them, edging forward in little hops from the exertion.

"Reach for the sky, Ellie," he says.

Ellie holds it for a second longer, like those old poodles on *The Ed Sullivan Show*, and then falls back down and wags her tail at having pulled it off.

"I need a Reason for Surrender," I say. "That's what we call it."

"Well, you're not going to get one," the guy says. He edges a wheel of his chair back and forth, turning him a little this way and that.

"Then I can't take the dog," I say.

"Then I'll just let her go when I get out the door," the guy says.

"If I were you I'd keep that dog," I say.

"If you were me you would've wheeled this thing off a bridge eleven years ago," the guy says. "If you were me you wouldn't be such a dick. If you were me you would've taken this dog, no questions asked."

We're at an impasse, this guy and me.

He lets go of Ellie's leash, and Ellie's covering all the corners of the office, sniffing. There's a woman in the waiting area behind him with a bullterrier puppy on her lap and the puppy's keeping a close eye on Ellie.

"Do you have any relatives or whatever who could take the dog?" I ask him.

The guy looks at me. "Do I sign something?" he says.

I can't help it, when I'm showing where to sign I can't keep the words back, I keep thinking of Ellie reaching for the sky: "It's better this way," I go. "We'll try and find her a home with someone equipped to handle her."

The guy doesn't come back at me. He signs the thing and hands me my pen and says, "Hey, Ellie. Hey, kid," and Ellie comes right over. He picks up her trailing leash and flops the end onto the counter where I can grab it, and then hugs her around the neck until she twists a little and pulls away.

"She doesn't know what's going on," I say.

He looks up at me, and I point, as if to say, Her.

The guy wheels the chair around and heads for the door. The woman with the bullterrier watches him go by with big eyes. I can't see his face, but it must be something. Ellie barks. There's no way to fix this.

I've got ASPCA pamphlets I've unboxed all over the counter. I've got impound forms to finish by today.

"Nobody's gonna want this dog," I call after him. I can't help it.

It's just me, now, at the counter. The woman stands up, holding the bullterrier against her chest, and stops, like she's not going to turn him over, like whatever her reasons, they may not be good enough.

Messiah

Right off we'll talk about it: people are (were) wrong about Macon. Macon this, Macon that, Macon's what's wrong with college football today. What Macon *is* is the best Corvair to run the football for State since God knows who, and some class-A studs have hauled leather there, Pops can tell you.

Pops says, It's like, you wanna back the Ferrari out of the garage, you gotta break some eggs.

Pops is one of the trainers. He handles ankles.

Macon I met on a recruiting visit. I was ass-kicker at defensive back, all-everything in Ohio, he was a fullback phenom from Jersey, one of those guys who scored nine thousand times a minute. We were flown in by the same alumnus. We were taken to the same restaurant. We were favored with the same jerky grins. We were told to stand in the middle of our prime rib and we were cheered by the crowd. Ever have a crowd cheer you in a restaurant?

Once we'd hunkered back to our meat I said my name and stuck my hand out. He looked at my hand and said, Messiah. I said, I beg your pardon? and he said, That's right, you *beg* my pardon.

We were both scout teamers at first. Scout team being Coach's idea of a way of using the freshmen, drop-goobers and general nose-pickers that infest a major college bench. What the scout team does is impersonate the upcoming opponent in practice and get its tiny brains beat out in the process. Neither Macon nor I intended to be on that little ride too long, but like Pops says, Caligula, he had to start somewhere.

It is something to see, trust me: every week two thousand or so come to see it.

So here's Macon, little Wilber Macon out of New Jersey of all places, having sewn MESSIAH on his back where his uppercase humble name should be and taking all sorts of radical verbal and physical abuse from the starters in pileups for his presumption in such matters, here's Macon coming back to the huddle with blood dripping from his nostrils like he's some sort of bull and then turning all sorts of savage, absolute maniac, and this being practice. Real officials work these practices—State saves money in all sorts of places but football is not one of them—and they were throwing flags at Macon like they were hoping they'd stick. Coach would take him out and talk to him, arm around his shoulder in the August heat, gruff but kind from the stands, but in your ear it was something like, Meat, you don't start producing out there and we are going to collectively plant your ass like an azalea and tamp down the soil.

So back in comes Macon, who goes wide on a sweep and tears through a linebacker and pops into the secondary expecting a big gain. You could see his eyes, big-gain eyes. Except Charlie Hall, starting monster man, cut his feet out from under him so that he went down like something hinged. Coach held his clipboard out for a flunky to take and then announced we'd run that play again. Not a radical nice thing to do, since the element of surprise was somewhat gone. Macon got stuffed big time, and the sound he made when hit was like the sound of someone beating a rug.

Which is where this starts to sound like *The Sports Book for Teens*: Macon, stung, pissed, lets fly on his final carry, coming out of his crouch like a psycho, a speedboat flipping, a ski jumper losing it, and is through a gap in the line before the hogs are up and set. It was terrifying, talent. We had seen a vision and some of us had to look away. Some of us saw but could not see. You could hear the whoosh of his breath on the sidelines and he lowered his helmet and stuck Jimmy Ford, as in starting weakside corner Gator Bowl MVP Jimmy Ford, such a shot that they heard the crack up in the practice towers. Jimmy let out what we call the dog yelp and went airborne with his face mask in pieces tumbling after. Macon kept going until he decided he wanted to stop. He carried Charlie Hall into the end zone and dropped the ball on his head.

So he started. He was, I wasn't. Specimen under the bridge, Pops said. Testing jokes were big that year. Everyone was pissing into bottles.

He not only started, he messed around at length with senior girls. He'd been on campus all of five weeks; they'd been on campus all of one. I couldn't find the student center. He had three different girls in three different dorms waiting up with the lights on, their hands on themselves, waiting for him to walk through that door.

This he told me.

The day he became a starter he took one girl into her room

and slapped her face over and over and over. The resident assistant came to the door and asked her if she was all right and she said she was. She was not but she said she was. I saw the swelling.

We opened against South Carolina. Dirty program, ugly uniforms, skaggy cheerleaders. They'd had another one of their nine-and-two-but-we-got-our-ass-kicked-by-the-good-team-in-the-bowl-game seasons, so they were underdogs, and deserved to be. I hoped we won big. I hoped to get in.

We were home. I lay in my bed from ten p.m. Friday night to seven a.m. Saturday morning and I did not unclench my fists. My roommate lay there on his side whispering, You fucker, you fucker, you fucker, for that same amount of time, his consonants sounding like the wind.

We got taped early. I got Pops. He handled my ankles and wrists like they were already broken and gone and he was going to miracle-ize them. I remember him pressing tape along my heel. I remember him aligning tape with my Achilles tendon. He squeezed and molded tape to my arches and instep and I believe I jumped higher and ran faster as a result.

I remember my locker, the steps of getting into the game uniform. I remember the cleats and the bright red rug. I remember the officials checking our pads. I remember the quiet before the tunnel. I remember the tunnel. I remember the run down that dark and hot and altogether soothing corridor into the light with the noise building until you hit cool air and nuthouse. We could not hear ourselves scream or touch pads and that was the way we wanted it. In the sunlight on that green rug we were deaf but could hear, were blind but could see. We wanted a part of whoever was nearby, South Carolina, the San Francisco 49ers, mad dogs. We were a natural disaster that moved in stages, a moment of misanthropy so pure we would have all dashed babies around on the ground and just kept on dashing.

We only mildly calmed down the whole first half. There were about sixty of us Denizens of the Depth Chart, as Pops called us, and we roamed and lined the sidelines, making treaties, breaking alliances, watching the game. Adding to the circus of TV cables, condenser dishes, Minicams, yard markers, drink and aid stations, whatever. We got in the way.

Some hotshot we'd seen all week on the films fumbled the opening kickoff and we scored right off. Our defense kept hitting like animals and by the half it was 26–0. Macon didn't see much of the ball. In the second half they came out and scored on some kind of half-assed reverse and the game ended that way, 26–7. So there was that clear locker-room division afterwards: the studs hunched over, spent, blue in spots and dripping, just really spent, and content, more content than we would ever be. Content to be there, content the hurting was over, content to have all that quality of stop. They sat there pulling at clammy tape like they were underwater and did not talk unless spoken to and sometimes not then. The rest of us bobbed back and forth like idiots in our fresh uniforms, wanting to go out on the town, show who we were or rather who we associated with, hurt people who weren't dressed as we were. We all listened to Coach. None of us in fresh uniforms gave interviews.

I took to following Macon, when I found him. Hazardous hobby, Pops said, and Pops knew. Macon the first night took me to bars where he sat alone, took me to the video store, took me to the 7-Eleven. Did he notice me? He did not let on, and I was good. The second night he took me to a girls' freshman dorm called Sweetwater and I watched him through a second-floor window dry hump a girl who under no circumstances appeared to want to be dry humped.

Did I do anything? I did not.

I followed him more. This I told Pops.

33

Pops said, It is definitively true that we as a country are producing a lesser breed of cat.

Pops said, Do you have a girlfriend?

I said, Are you named after Louis Armstrong?

Pops said Armstrong could not hit. Armstrong could not stick. This we laughed at. I would not, I realized, tell him that I wanted to see what Macon did when I followed him.

And did Macon know? What about the night he maneuvered the girl over to the window, got her there when it could not have been easy and could not have been necessary? What about the night I lost him crossing the quad and found him again standing under the streetlight, hands bouncing in jacket pockets?

What about the night he had the girl under the arch by the wrist and let her go, so that she walked and then ran past me, where I was waiting?

And how did I get to start? Macon made me a spot.

In practice after our second game, Macon found the strong-side corner strung out and exposed after having absorbed the block from the guard and Macon put the crown of his helmet into the earhole of our strong-side corner's helmet so that the strong-side corner's head went one way and his body went another. The strong-side corner's name was Jeff Voight. The cheerleaders turned away as a group. I myself thought he was dead. I thought, He's dead, and I'm starting. Someone orbiting the earth would have known it was his neck. This was confirmed very slowly by eleven medical staffers who finally removed him the way you'd pick up a finished jigsaw puzzle. While this was happening Macon was ranging up and down the sideline waiting, and my adrenaline was heading around the block, my college career about to begin.

So this Jeff Voight had a big scare but is now all right. He had as well a lot of friends on the defense and they were all now intensely interested in Macon in practice, and the hitting went from absurd to a little out of hand. They rode him in pileups. While people untangled they pulled hair from his calves. They poked fingers through his face mask, searching for eyes.

The head terrorizer of this group was our weakside linebacker, Billy Jeter, who'd been Jeff Voight's best friend. Mr. Jeter and I took Macon down on a swing pass and Mr. Jeter got up by standing on Macon's ankles. Macon said, and I quote: Next play, motherfucker, you get yours.

This was like Ruth calling his shot. Who knew the play would send him in Jeter's direction, and who knew if sent whether he could truly and permanently hurt Jeter? But both of these came to pass, Macon revving up, getting a nice start on a pitch, coming out all helmet and knees, and clawing up one side of Jeter and down the other. Jeter had both hands on his chest like a grandmother in distress and he was right to do so because he had a cracked sternum and his football career was now over.

This, maybe, Macon did for us.

So here is how I played, as a starter in week three for State in 1989: well. I was mesmerized out there at first, reacting too late to the snap and flow, but got it in gear for part two and started hitting, and things, as Pops said, turned out all right. People were much bigger at this level, so that I was frequently trampled and not infrequently felt like something in the spin cycle when I tangled with the big meat inside, but they were no meaner than I was, nor more willing to hurt, and this for me seemed a kind of grace.

We won games we were supposed to win. We lost one we were supposed to lose. While that was happening Coach took off his watch and jumped up and down on it on the sidelines. Charlie

Hall behind me said, There's Coach killing time again, and the goobers on the bench laughed and slapped their pads like members of the team.

Claudia was my ethical dilemma. Claudia was my moral choice. Claudia was in my Many Faces of Man class and she had only been kind, to me and to most others. When the professor had said, Mr. Proekopp, you aren't with us, are you? Claudia had said, Is the idea here that the football players can't keep up?

Claudia I could have wanted to go out with. Claudia I introduced to Macon, at a mixer. She liked him. I followed them around the party. I followed them home. At her door he kissed her sweetly goodnight. At his door he whistled and hooted. I knew he would see her again.

In practice his eyes were unreadable in the heavy shadow under the helmet. Our big game was this week: conference rival and interstate matchup. Every day I went home trailing equipment behind me, watching Macon disappear in his direction, thinking, Tonight? Monday and Wednesday I sat next to Claudia and talked about everything that would not help. Thursday night he led me out and around the campus, the full tour, Macon the director of nighttime admissions, always fifty yards ahead, slowing down faintly at points of particular interest. When we got to Claudia's he went inside without hesitation. From the base of a tree I watched her fourth-floor window. But the light was a yellow blank, and they appeared in the lobby, came out, and started walking. We walked everywhere. I trailed, the tail of the kite. By a doughnut shop they kissed and I rubbed the glass of a bookstore window with my cheek. They passed a park and sat beside a series of bike racks. They ended in the arboretum.

In the darkness I lost them. I blundered along. I left the path. I did not call her name. I stepped on glass which crunched underfoot. By a tree I found her, kneeling. Her arms were behind her. Her head was back and her pants were open, though there was only a white triangle of belly in that light. Macon was behind her. Macon was holding her that way. Macon had convinced her to be silent.

Even with her head back she could see me. I could not tell what her eyes intended to communicate. I could not tell how long they had been there like that. I could tell she was not going anywhere. I could tell they could both see something in my face that I could not.

Spending the Night
with the Poor

I was at the Plattsburgh Dance Studio for like thirty seconds before I realized it was a rip-off. I even went back outside like I'd
dropped a mitten or something, but my mother was already gone.
I could see her taillights two stoplights down. She was the only
Isuzu in a pack of pickups with gun racks.

The facilities were terrible. It was in a warehouse. The wooden
floor ran out at one point and whoever was on that side was supposed to dance on cement. I was like, No thank you, and wherever they wanted to arrange me, I made sure I ended up back on
the good side.

The teacher was clearly unqualified. It was supposed to be a
musical theater course, six weeks, and it turned out she hadn't
been in anything. "She probably just owns the records," Crystal
whispered while we stood there freezing. There was no heat. Ms.
Adams—she stressed the "Ms."—gave us her Opening Day
speech. It had to do with getting to Broadway one step at a time.

I was embarrassed for her. When she finished, she looked disappointed that we didn't all cheer and carry her around the room on our shoulders. We just stood there warming our hands in our armpits.

She asked if there were questions. "Do we have any *heat?*" I asked, and Crystal gave me an elbow and I gave her one back. She loved it.

At the back of the room a *Threepenny Opera* poster was taped to a sawhorse. Pathetic.

"Is that a *Cats* sweatshirt?" I asked Ms. Adams. The way she said it was, you could see she didn't get it.

"You're terrible," Crystal said.

Crystal was the reason I stayed at all. Nobody asked, but I told my mother that night that it was horrible, and told her why. She said what she always said—Well, Give It a Little Time. I didn't argue. Not because I thought it would get better, but because of Crystal, and because what else did I have to do? Sit around staring at my brother?

Crystal was so poor. I knew most of the kids would be pretty low class, but it was either this or voice lessons and I really wanted to do this. Crystal was poor like in the movies. She carried her stuff in a plastic bag. She brought a little Tupperware thing of Coke instead of buying them from the machine. She was clueless about her hair; she had it up with a butterfly clip, like Pebbles. She wore blue eye shadow. And she was pretty anyway. She had a good smile and a mouth like Courtney Love's.

She *walked* to the school, every day. We met twice a week, after regular school: Mondays and Fridays. It was like a mile and a half. Her parents had one car and her dad needed it. She had two pairs of socks total, one gray ragg, one a pair of guy's sweat socks with the stripes across the top. Her coat she got from a place called the Women's Exchange. Her older brother was retarded.

"So's mine," I told her.

He isn't but he might as well be.

She said her father worked in an office. I didn't say anything.

That Friday we were helping each other stretch and she said, "So are you a little rich or way rich?" I told her my family wasn't exactly going bankrupt. It was a good way to put it. I told her what my dad did. I told her where we lived.

"Good for you," she said, like she meant it.

I told her I was going to keep ragging on her socks until she got new ones.

"Oh, *that's* funny," she said, meaning that they were ragg socks.

But that next Monday she had different ones, and we didn't say anything about it. When we were getting ready to go I told her I was going to help her.

"Oh, yeah?" she said, yawning. She yawned so wide her eyes teared up. "How?"

I told her I'd been thinking about it all Sunday night.

"That's really great," she said. You could see she thought I was going to give her a Mounds bar or something.

I told her that since I was a foot taller I had a lot of clothes I'd outgrown or I wasn't using. Nothing was totally cheesy or worn out. Like this forest-green top I completely loved but wouldn't fit me anymore. Or this wool skirt that was Catholic school–looking but okay.

"Please," she said, and we rolled our eyes and laughed.

There was more stuff, too. I named other things and even threw in some things I did want. I always do stuff like that and afterwards regret it.

We were standing around the lobby of the building. It was cold from everyone coming and going, but at least it was out of the wind. I was wearing a man's wool overcoat I really loved and a

41

fur-lined winter cap my mom called smart, but so what? When you got through all of that it was still just me.

We were just standing around waiting, looking at different things.

"Listen," she said. "Doesn't your mother want you to hang on to your stuff, or give it to a relative?"

"My mother doesn't care," I said. That wasn't really true. But I figured that later, when Crystal found out, she'd be even more grateful.

I didn't bring her anything on Friday, though. I had the stuff ready and I just left it in my room. While my mom drove me there, I thought, Why couldn't you just *bring* it?

"You are so stupid," I thought. I realized I'd said it out loud. My mother turned to me. "What?" she said.

I was embarrassed. I was sitting there turning colors, probably.

"Why are you stupid?" she said.

"How do you know I wasn't talking about you?" I said.

She smiled. "The way you said it," she said.

I had no answer for that.

"Why are you stupid?" she asked again.

"Why do you think?" I finally said.

"Don't snap at me," she said. "All right? I don't need it."

When we got there I got out of the car and slammed the door. I saw her face when she drove off and I thought this was what always happened; I made everyone feel bad for no reason.

Crystal was waiting for me on the good end of the dance floor. She'd saved a space by spreading her stuff out. I was still mad. She saw how I looked, so she was all ears with Ms. Adams. She didn't say anything and neither did I.

We ended early because Ms. Adams had a dentist's appointment. She told us about the periodontal work she needed to have done like we wanted to hear. Then she left. I felt like I'd just gotten there. Everyone else called their rides. My mother, of course, was still out. She hadn't even gotten home yet. I left a message on the machine. My brother was probably right there and didn't bother to pick up.

Crystal said she'd wait with me. Which was nice of her, though all she had to look forward to was a walk home anyway. I told her we'd give her a ride when my mom came.

We talked about how much we hated the class. The ad said we would do Sondheim and stuff. So far we'd been working through the chorus of "Some Enchanted Evening." According to Ms. Bad Gums, that was so we could get to know our voices.

"I already know my voice," Crystal always said, like she didn't want to know it any better.

She shared some Hershey's Kisses, which looked pretty old. The foil was faded. She told me she liked my Danskin. I told her she had great calves. She said she worked out every night, watching TV. The conversation kind of hung there.

"Have you thought about doing something with your hair?" I asked.

"Have you thought about doing something with your mouth?" she said back, meaning I was a wiseass, which was what my mother and brother always said. "You bitch," I said, and she said, "It takes one to know one," which was true.

She showed me how to look back behind the vending machines where the money rolled and people couldn't get to it. We found fifty cents and got a Reese's. I had money but I hung on to it.

When my mother finally drove up it was totally dark. Two of the big lights were out in front of the building. She beeped the horn and we ran from the lobby to the car.

"Where were you?" I said, and she gave me one of her I'm-not-going-to-dignify-that-with-a-response looks.

"Who's this?" she said.

"Crystal," I said.

"*Crys*tal?" my mother said. She let it go at that.

"Can you take me to my dad's office instead?" Crystal asked.

"Sure," I said.

She gave my mother directions. She made zero small talk. I couldn't see her face.

We dropped her off. The office was a factory that made brake linings. I waved through the window. My mother pulled back into traffic.

"It's not such a horrible name," I said. I was sulking.

"It's a pretty horrible name," my mother said. "But it's only a name."

The next day I got the pile of clothes back together. It ended up filling a lawn bag. My mom came upstairs and asked what I was doing.

I told her. She sat on the bed. She watched for a little while. She said things like, "You want to get rid of *that?*"

"Is your friend going to take this the right way?" she said. "Did you tell her you were going to do this?"

I told her yes. She smiled. This was another one of her daughter's stupid ideas.

"Well, don't go crazy," she finally said. She got up and went downstairs.

Immediately my brother wandered into my room. I'm supposed to have privacy but it's like a train station.

"Get out of here," I said. "I don't go in your room."

"What do you want from me?" he said. "Go in my room."

I didn't let him see what was in the bag.

He had my stuffed Snoopy from when I was little by the ears and he was pounding its forehead on the headboard. "Whaddaya doing?" he said. "Giving your clothes to the less fortunate?"

"None of your business," I said. Then I said, "Like you'd ever do anything for anybody."

"Why don't you do a telethon?" he said.

I got a book off my shelf and read until he left.

I complained about him to my mother and she reminded me he was going through a tough time. He had seven things he went out for his first year in high school and didn't get into any.

On Monday I told Crystal about him. I said, "Maybe we're both losers," meaning him and me.

"I doubt it," she said.

I'd left the bags of clothes home again. "I was going to bring the clothes this time," I finally said when we were getting ready to go.

"I should give *you* something," Crystal said.

"Oh, you don't have to do that," I said. What was she going to give me? Something she whittled?

She asked if I wanted to stay over Friday night.

"Sure," I said.

"Give me your number," she said, and I gave her a number.

I have like three friends, and they never call. They had to be practically dragged to my birthday party.

It was okay with my mother. "I am going to have a drink," she said, when I asked her what she thought. I told her it was Crystal, the girl she met. "I assumed," she said.

Later we ran it by my father, up in his study. Somebody on his team had totally screwed up a deposition, so he had to make another whole trip to someplace like Iowa. He asked who Crystal was. He said it was fine with him. "Spending the night with the poor," he said, and he gave me a hug.

"Very nice," my mother said to herself as we came back downstairs.

That Friday I loaded the lawn bag into the trunk. My mother

45

would pick us up after the lessons and take us to Crystal's, and then pick me up Saturday afternoon after some errands.

Crystal was nervous in class. She was fidgety afterwards, waiting for my mother. I was flattered.

My mother was right on time, which I told Crystal wouldn't happen in a million years. "How are you, Mrs. Gerwig?" she said when she got in the car.

"I'm fine, Crystal," my mom said. "How about you?"

Crystal said she was fine, too.

"It's nice of your parents to invite Lynn over," my mother told her once we pulled onto the highway.

"I so love the twilight this time of year, don't you?" Crystal said back. I almost lost it.

We got off at the Riverside exit. I didn't know anyone lived down there, poor or not. All you could see from the highway was oil tanks.

Crystal gave directions while my mom turtled along like the whole thing was a trap. I kept hoping the houses wouldn't get any worse.

"Mom, the gas pedal. On the right," I said.

My mother just drove.

We were all quiet.

"Right here," Crystal said.

I peeped out of my window. What was I scared of? There weren't going to be enough cable channels?

On the way there I'd told myself that there wouldn't be anything so terrible about the house. I was wrong. It was a long white trailer. It had a yellow stripe. There were empty plastic buckets around the front porch. Something rusty was half buried in the yard. My mother pulled up so even the car wasn't too close to the curb. Her face was fine.

When she got out of the car Crystal's dad came out of the house. He looked like any other dad. He had on a Nirvana T-shirt. While they said hello I got the keys from my mom's hand and opened the trunk. I pulled out the bag and lugged it to the front door.

Her dad's name was Tom.

"Where you goin' with that?" her dad said.

"Lynn's givin' me some clothes," Crystal said. "The ones that don't fit her anymore."

My mother was wincing. Like Crystal and her father were blind.

I was still at the front door of the trailer. I could see people inside.

"It's just a lot of weird stuff, Dad," Crystal said.

"Hey, I don't care," Crystal's dad said. "If it's all right with Lynn's mother here," he said.

"It's fine with me," my mother said. After a second she crossed the yard to give me a hug. She looked at me. "You behave yourself," she said. She got back in the car and drove off.

"So what're we havin' for dinner?" Crystal's dad said.

"We should have hot dogs," Crystal said.

We all went in the house.

Her mother and her retarded brother were in the living room with the shades down, watching TV. I thought it was weird that her mother hadn't come out.

"Nice to meet you," I told them.

They were both fat, but not hugely fat. The brother had black hair combed sideways and his eyes were half closed. I couldn't tell if that was part of the way he was retarded or if he was just sleepy. His mother had next to her the biggest ashtray on earth. It was wider than the lamp table it was on.

Crystal said I should get the bag from the porch. She told them while I went to get it that I'd given her this huge bag of clothes. They were looking at me when I came back in.

"Merry Christmas!" I said, because I couldn't think of anything else. I put it on the rug in front of the TV.

The house smelled. There were dirty coffee cups on the windowsill. I had my hands flat against my thighs.

Her father poked in from the kitchen and said, "What's in the bag?" but then didn't wait to find out. He called he was starting dinner.

Her brother dug around in the bag. Her mother watched. I still didn't know his name. I was still standing by the front door. Crystal felt bad at the way things were going but I couldn't do anything to help her feel better.

"So what's in there?" she said, like everything was okay. It was horrible.

Her brother pulled out stuff I didn't even remember throwing in. Some things I could still wear, and a blue velvet dress.

"Oh," her mother said, when her brother held up the dress.

A *Penthouse* magazine was lying around in plain sight. The room was cold and everyone was bundled up. You could smell sweat. The kitchen was on one side and they had framed pictures of Crystal and her brother around the door leading to the other rooms. It was a longer trailer than it looked.

The kitchen was clean. We ate in there, watching the TV on the counter. I looked every so often at the floors and the ceiling, and Crystal caught me at it.

We had pound cake for dessert. Her father and brother got into a fight about how much her brother could have.

Afterwards we hung out in Crystal's room. It was across from her mom and dad's. Her brother was going to sleep on the sofa. I thanked her parents for the very nice dinner, even though I hadn't seen her mother do anything. They said we should get ready for bed soon.

That was fine with me. It was about 7:30.

Her half of the room was neat. She had a throw rug, and her bed was made, with some books arranged big to small on a bookshelf in the headboard. Her brother's side was filthy. You could see that she'd tried to pick up. There were loose Oreos in some slippers under the dresser.

"You can sleep on my bed," Crystal said.

A poster of a muscle car flapped out from the ceiling over her brother's bed, like a sail. I told her I could sleep over there, but she said no.

I was still standing in the middle of the room. I didn't want to be there, and she knew it.

"Do you want to see some of my books, or play a game?" she said. "I got Clue."

"Okay," I said.

She didn't move. She sat on her brother's bed. I sat on hers. I smelled soap.

"Should we go to bed?" I finally said. She shrugged, looking down at my feet.

We brushed our teeth and got into our nightgowns. Even the water tasted weird. I was glad I brought my own towel. We called goodnight down the hall and got into bed. Then she had to get up to turn off the light. She got into bed again. The parking garage across the street lit up the whole room.

"Are you having an okay time?" she said, from her brother's bed.

"Yeah," I said. She shifted around on her back. They were watching some kind of travelogue in the living room and we both lay there, listening to it. I think she felt so bad she couldn't even ask them to turn it down.

"My cousin Katie has so much money," she said.

"Did you hear me?" she said.

"What am I supposed to say?" I said.

She sighed. It was like a bubble filling the house, pressing on my ears. I hated it there.

"I don't know why I say some things," she said. She started to cry.

"Are you crying?" I said. "What are you crying for?"

It just made her cry to herself. I hadn't asked very nicely.

"Why are you crying?" I said.

"Oh," she said, like she was going to answer, but she didn't.

We both lay there. I made a disgusted noise. I breathed in her smell on the pillow. She was quiet after that. The travelogue went off. I wondered if her brother had to stay up until her parents went to bed.

It was so bright in the room I could read my watch. When it was 11:30 I said, "I should go."

"What do you want from me?" she said, exactly the way my brother does.

I got up and got dressed without turning on the light. "I should use the phone," I said. She was still on her back.

I went out into the hall. The house was dark. The phone was in the kitchen. My mother answered on the second ring. I kept my voice down. I was worried she was going to make me explain, but she didn't. She said, "Are you all right?" Then she said my father would come.

It would take about a half hour. I had to wait. I hung up and went back into the bedroom and shut the door. "My father's coming," I said.

"Fine," Crystal said. She was sitting up. "You want the light on?"

"No," I said.

We sat there. I thought about the way I'd thought of her the night before. The night before I'd thought she needed beauty in her life.

"Take your clothes with you when you go," she said.

"This is totally me. I'm just being weird," I said.

I was going to quit the classes the next day by phone. If she tried to call me she'd find out the number I'd given her was fake. Like we said when a total dork asked for our number: I gave him my faux number. And she'd think I couldn't deal with her being so poor. She wouldn't realize it was everything else I couldn't deal with. I knew I deserved exactly what I got, all the rest of my life. And when I was stuck with her in her bedroom I didn't want her to deserve any more, either. But before that, for a little while, I wanted good things for her; I wanted to make her life a little better. I wanted to make her think, That Lynn—that Lynn's a nice girl. And wasn't that worth something?

Atomic Tourism

Ahead of them a eucalyptus tree was split open to the root, the trunk sections curled back like the peels of a banana. The eucalyptus smell filled the air.

"You may think you figured on all of this, but we're a long way from business as usual," Tinderlee said. They turned off the road with a little jounce for emphasis and eased around a shattered car blocking the road like a tipped dumpster. Tinderlee's hands were light on the wheel, and the sun glazed and burned the windshield. Above them in a black willow tree something skittered from branch to branch.

His wife refused to answer. She sat upright and touched her hand to the dash to steady herself. A fine, silken dust, the color of coffee with cream, covered the upholstery, from the open window and the long hours on this turnoff.

"I'm not saying I figured on it, exactly," she finally said, not especially upset. "I'm saying it could have been avoided. You got

me here reading the map and you don't listen to what I say. This
road ends in a crater and the last road ended in a crater and it's
plain to me we never should have gotten off ten."

She turned her head from him, as if speaking for the record. "I
said we should've come up through the middle, but no, you
wanted to see Tallahassee. Well, here's Tallahassee. Craters so
wide you could run a marching band through one end and not
wake a sleeping cat on the other side. Here's Tallahassee."

They were listing slightly on the shoulder of Florida 319, just
outside of Bellair, the Airstream behind their Buick a glittering
fat tube in the sun. A lizard inched across the road and seemed to
expire just short of the double yellow line, rolling onto its side, its
tiny jaws slack and visible.

"Look at that," Amanda said. "That's me. We should've had
iced tea and we should've been in Georgia by now."

Tinderlee made a face and eased the car into gear again.
Ahead of them in the hot distance the scrub pine lining the road
leaned away from the crater, a great lip of dirt and flat, ripped
pavement. It looked a good ways across. On the other side what
Tinderlee assumed had been Bellair looked as if it had been
stamped to pieces in some kind of cosmic tantrum and the rubble dusted with sand and ash. They could make out black areas,
things charred or shadowed, here and there in the sun. A single
flagpole stood in abject definition near the center. Hawks
wheeled high above with a kind of patient optimism.

He took a last look, but Amanda seemed uninterested. He
turned the Buick in a wide arc across the road, its tires crunching
and popping slowly on the gravel shoulder.

He said something amiable about having room to turn.

"I'm just so happy about it I could spit biscuits," Amanda said.

Tinderlee chose to ignore her. If she was going to ruin her own
day, that was her business. "No harm done," he said.

54

"That," she said, pointing to the Geiger counter, "hasn't regis-
tered a thing since Orlando. I wouldn't be knocked over with a
feather if we been keeping watch on a dead machine."

The Geiger counter sat unsteady and accused on the seat between them.

It didn't matter, Tinderlee said. The Airstream straightened
out behind them and they picked up speed, Bellair diminishing
in the rearview mirror. Some of the craters had grass growing in
them already. They reminded him of golf courses in spots.

But Amanda was silent, and remained so during the loop
around Tallahassee.

"You had big plans for the CB, too, I recall," she finally said.
"Now for all the good it'll do us, we might as well turn on the radio."

Tinderlee smiled at a curve ahead. He said, "You sure carry on
when you don't get to stop every five feet."

Amanda cracked a Coors. She took a sip and said, "Well, I
don't know what put a song in your heart."

Amanda wanted to see Atlanta. She'd seen it once, years before, and she wanted to see it now. Atlanta had been hit by four
different warheads at three different times, she had heard. All of
them near misses. A man in an Eldorado they'd met at a rest stop
outside of Winter Garden had told them stories about the size of
the devastated areas. He'd described mountainous jungles of rubble, highway overpasses twisted back upon themselves. Amanda
had edged forward on the picnic bench, intrigued. She had decided she wanted Before and After pictures.

Tinderlee kept up some patter supporting his side of things, as
the miles reeled by and they made good time heading south
along areas that seemed unaffected. He said it would be a shame
and a sin to have been right here and not to have seen what there
was to see. They followed 319 down through Sopchoppy and

stopped for a look-see near a rubbish dump as big as a small town. They dawdled on a bridge over the Ochlockonee. In snags and eddies dead fish were as thick as cobblestones, slick and silver. The smell was intense. An occasional bird wing rose above the mass. Tinderlee pointed out an unusual grayish scum lining the riverbank in spots, riding wavelets like egg white on water.

They saw Dog Island and Carrabelle and Port St. Joe. They saw Spanish moss reduced to cinders, and a chicken that had been blown into a power line. It hung there with wings outspread, featherlight in the wind. They took 71 to avoid Panama City and headed north. "We never go where I want to go," Amanda said. "I could talk until my teeth shrivel in my gums and we wouldn't go where I want to go."

They were going to Enterprise, Alabama. The slightest vibration or quirk in a gyroscopic package the size of a football had deflected an SS-18 bound for Montgomery to a spot some seventy-five miles south, in a field just east of Enterprise. The SS-18 had carried a twenty-megaton warhead and had been set for groundburst, and Enterprise had been covered with red Alabama clay like a castle in a child's sandbox. The blast had been seen in Tampa. The crater that remained had not been accurately measured. Tinderlee heard estimates of depth reaching six hundred feet. Think of it, he said at a rest stop outside of Marianna. Amanda chewed silently on a cucumber sandwich. He struggled to find a simile. It was like having a chance to be one of the first people to see something, he said. It was like being one of the first people to see the Grand Canyon.

They stopped for gas when they could, filling jerry cans as well as the tank. Gas prices varied at the whim of the attendant, and most stations weren't selling at all. Where gas was available, the station displayed a green flag. Tinderlee pulled into a Pina station that had huge and ragged rats nailed in a row across the front of its garage, and the attendant eyed him suspiciously.

The fill-up set them back a hundred and five dollars. Even so, Tinderlee pointed out, you save for a trip, not on one. The attendant was won over by Tinderlee's good nature and allowed that the crater near Enterprise was something to see. He suggested they visit Childersburg, as well. It had been in the fallout pattern of Birmingham and really took a dumping. It was completely covered with ash.

The attendant went on to say that he'd had a cousin who'd been up in Washington years ago when that mountain went off, and the cousin had told him that it was exactly the same thing, to see this town. But exactly.

They thanked him and pledged to check it out. When they pulled back onto the road Amanda said, "I wouldn't go there if it was the last place on earth."

Outside Dothan they ate lunch at a picnic area. Another traveler sat a few tables over. He was a middle-aged man with a flat belly and he was wearing a blue-and-yellow Navy commander's cap with oak leaves on the brim. A lot of people, they noticed, had done some casual looting.

The three of them were cautious at first but soon hit it off like old friends, and the fellow, whose name was Rick Bozack, came over to their table and shared a six of Michelob Light. He was just finishing something like the circuit they were on. They felt closer to him for the coincidence. He'd been to the Enterprise crater and recommended it. He passed on a tip or two concerning the best view, which was from the north rim.

He was heading down to see the new bay. The Russians had lobbed a warhead of indeterminate size into the Gulf of Mexico, producing a wave that swept from Panama City to Corpus Christi in an arc. The water had never really receded, and the Gulf had been enlarged by a good twenty percent or so as a result. New Orleans and Corpus Christi and everything else in the way had disappeared in the bargain.

Tinderlee and Amanda responded politely to his enthusiasm but privately thought the idea pretty foolish. They'd ruled out a look at the bay a long time ago. Why would it look any different from any other bay? It was like going to see a flower bed after four feet of snow, Amanda said.

But Rick Bozack kept on, talking about his old life (he'd sold incubators and heart and kidney machines out of Indianapolis). He told a funny story concerning three foxhounds he'd seen squabbling on some lawn furniture. He pressed his fingertips to his gums experimentally. There was a lot of white scalp beneath the mesh of his cap.

What killed him were these dreams he kept having, he said.

Tinderlee looked at Amanda.

Did they have any problems like that? Bozack asked.

Tinderlee said they didn't.

They were quiet after that. Bozack didn't say boo. The wind rustled papers in a garbage can behind them.

He dreamed about the first day, Bozack said. Here it was years later and he still dreamed about that first day.

They finished their lunch. "So what happened on the first day?" Amanda asked politely.

Rick Bozack smiled. "Hey, I don't mean to be a conversation stopper," he said. "It's just that it stays with me."

Tinderlee said it was probably some story.

"It is," Rick Bozack said. "A humdinger."

"I'd like to hear it," Amanda said.

"I was south of Omaha, on a 737," Rick Bozack said. "We were going from New Orleans to Minneapolis and the plane shook like somebody hit it with a strap."

He held up an empty Michelob bottle and shook it as a visual aid.

"We had the entire Joffrey Ballet or something in first class, and they'd been piling up the little hooch bottles pretty good. They were drunk. It was a party. Then bam: we dropped ten thousand feet in a minute and a half. Everybody thought it was the end of the line. Screaming, bug eyes, the works. But here's what killed me: we bottomed out and the dancers were still laughing. The pilot came on and said that it seemed there'd been some sort of concussion to the northeast, and we couldn't raise Omaha. We couldn't raise St. Louis, either. We couldn't raise anybody. He didn't tell us that our Boeing was coming apart at the seams. He brought us around in a forty-five-degree bank like he was back with the Hellcats in the Navy, and the next thing we knew we were skimming waves of corn and he was drawling something nobody could hear and we were all screaming and holding on to padded seats like they were going to save us. We ended up making it, though a wheel collapsed and I remember cups flying the length of the plane. A stewardess went from seat to seat telling us to take off our shoes and use the emergency slides, and to keep running when we hit the ground, in case of explosion. She had an egg of a bump on her forehead and I remember thinking, *There's* a headache in the morning."

Rick Bozack cleared his throat and arranged the beer bottles in front of him. He talked about the drumroll of shoes hitting the floor, the emergency doors blowing outward, the yellow slides inflating like wings.

He said, "But I remember the dancers, still laughing in first class. In the aisles they pushed and shoved like kids at recess. They pirouetted and made little leaps and the stewardesses kept saying 'Walk, please; walk.' They made those little leaps one by one onto the slide, laughing, the rest of the group cheering each leap. The rest of us crowded into the aisles behind them in shock. When we got into the cornfield I grabbed hold of an older woman who was having trouble with the stalks and we ran breaking through the corn like fullbacks. The dancers were way ahead of us and we only heard them because the corn was too high. They were laughing. We heard them, and saw them sometimes when they jumped."

When they jumped, Rick Bozack said, their upraised arms would float above the tassels of the corn and disappear, and their laughter would stay with everybody else running along behind.

After a minute he fixed his posture and clinked his bottles together musically. He looked a little embarrassed. Anyway, he still dreamed about it, he said. Amanda smiled.

In the car later they discussed his story. Tinderlee liked the dancers in the cornfield, but Amanda wondered if the whole thing hadn't been a big buildup for a fizzle. They dropped the issue after that, staring out over their sides of the road. They'd left Rick Bozack, waving and looking more than a little hangdog, back at the rest stop. They'd wished him luck on the trip.

"Thanks," he had said. "Luck."

The crater they found at Enterprise was more than they could have imagined. It was stupefying. They stood there looking into the hole and then at its walls in the distance. Amanda's jaw went a little slack. The whole thing was wild, impossible, otherworldly. In the great strata of rock below they made out shapes: a duck, a horse, Cuba. A lightning bolt, hundreds of feet wide.

They had it all to themselves. A devastated tree with splintered branches on the opposite lip indicated scale.

Moss grew in great patches on nearby rocks. A vast silence

hung over the pit. Tinderlee could make out toward the bottom garbage that people had thrown in.

The breeze picked up. Amanda went back to the car for her jacket. They followed a path a few hundred feet down from the top and gave up. Water was collecting at the very bottom into a lake.

They stayed on in the fading light until Amanda said she'd had enough of holes in the ground to last her a lifetime. Then they walked back up the path, mum as zombies, got into the Buick, and headed east for Atlanta.

They stopped to sleep by the side of the road. In the Airstream, Tinderlee lay on his back, his joints aching like old bursitis. He was looking through the little window at the night sky, beautiful and clear, and the stars beyond.

"I wonder where Rick Bozack is now," he said. Amanda shifted in the darkness, next to him.

"I was just thinking the same thing," she murmured.

The rain beat down on them in a fury the next morning all the way through western Georgia, encouraging their silence and not letting up until they were nearing Atlanta itself. The Geiger counter sputtered and acted up fitfully. Tinderlee was stiff and melancholy and Amanda kept to herself, sucking noisily on a peach pit.

When the sun finally came out, she sighed and said, "Maybe we should cut this trip short. Maybe we've done enough."

"Maybe," Tinderlee said.

They rested up and showered at a Days Inn still in business in McDonough, though that set them back more than they would have liked. They were on the road again by 9:30. Neither wanted any breakfast. They were both still quiet.

They approached the city limits. Tinderlee had to thread his way through the mess like a penitent drunk on the way home.

They spent part of the last leg on an interstate, creeping past the hulks of jackknifed trailer trucks strewn across the lanes like geometric boulders.

They got off an intact exit and drove toward the downtown, bumping along shoulders and climbing onto sidewalks to keep going. At an intersection a traffic light hung down at windshield level like a baleful electronic guard. On one side of another block the office buildings had collapsed into the street in a great slide of concrete and glass and steel.

They took the Buick a little farther before having to stop, the Airstream hitch grinding and hanging up on a tentlike fracture in the pavement.

They walked a good ways after that. Tinderlee consulted a map he'd dug out of the wreck of a store. It flapped in the wind. They climbed rubble that gave way with dull sounds beneath their feet. They passed neighborhoods of debris. It was like an endless junkyard. Far off, the breeze was banging something metal against something else. They found an undamaged fire hydrant, and an open umbrella with a rainbow pattern centered on a traffic island. Amanda puzzled over a dog's leash and collar still tied to a parking meter. The empty collar when she lifted it swayed near her head like a thought balloon.

They kept walking, the banging sound persistent in the distance.

Finally Amanda turned an ankle. They stopped. She got sick on her hands and knees over a grate. Tinderlee bent over her. Their breathing was getting noisier.

He set his compass on a piece of concrete and told Amanda that as far as he could tell they were either in the downtown area or had just passed through it.

She was listing over to one side. Her hair moved against her cheek. She was very pale. "Did you notice the bugs?" she said.

Tinderlee said he had. "City of bugs, now," he added.

She smiled. He realized her sadness, and understood she'd been sad, all along.

"I'm not so good," she said. "All those rems and rads."

He nodded. He squatted beside her. They both looked at their hands.

"Where should we go after this?" she asked.

"I don't know," he said. On a side street a sheet or shirt sleeve fluttered like someone waving. "Maybe take a rest."

"That'd be good," she said finally. She seemed to want to do something with one hand and they watched it move around her lap. She started to say something else and stopped.

He got up to see to her comfort, and she said, "Look," her voice full of everything that was gone. She was pointing at the crushed wall of a bank. The letters EDERAL SAVINGS were still intact, the brick blackened, the whitish silhouette of a figure with its arms crossed before its face fixed on the black surface like a photographic negative.

Who We Are,
What We're Doing

People off base used to tell us like we wouldn't know that flying
the hottest jets, the screamers, was the hardest thing in the world.
We're just boys, we're all of us just boys, from Sioux City, Ala-
mogordo, Madison, Tulsa. This is war and who's been trained for
these things, really, in peacetime? Our wingleader tells us, Hell,
muffins, around here your lives are on the line just buckling into
the cockpit. You know your checklists? You Intimate with your
Information? We're talking night skies of indicators and vistas of
switches. Twitch the wrong way, catch a sleeve, trip a switch, and
in milliseconds you're over on your back and flat into the scree.
Our wingleader is speaking here we should say of the hot jets, the
serious animals, flathead F-15s with their ordnance overload
spread behind them in hangars like the whole toybox emptied, F-
18s swept and grooved and windtunneled like the last sports car.
Our wingleader says stand close when they're running up the engines, and feel the tarmac ripple under your feet: nothing any-

where is more kick-ass get pumped overpowered. I'm in the slot and he's right: on scramble takeoffs the canopy's trembling and shaking and the inlet ducts are howling and the little position and formation lights are winking those tiny piercing lights and my weapons officer behind me points to the DEADEYE on his helmet and waggles his fingers and gives me a thumbs-up, and nothing in this world looks more ready than we do to move past control and do lamentable things to everything in the vicinity. It's better than family, it's better than sex with strangers, it's better than movies.

And the secret is, nothing's easier. Take the Eagle off the runway, straighten it out, keep an eye peeled for ECM, and cruise climb up as part of the diamond—it's like working the microwave, running the VCR. The automated systems and combat tactics keep everything within the envelope, as approved by engineers, and at times it's like you're just a passenger. R and D's been working on the foolproof for years, and somewhere along the line things got so hard they got easy.

What's hard our wingleader says is *employing* these overdesigned animals, turning them into Ragin' Cajuns in the nuthouse of air-to-air mix-ups, inducing them to pacify the mystery blips and hostiles. When we find somebody "dogfight" is the right word for it: it's ragged and nasty and it beats you up. Eagles pulling eight g's stick you with eight times the force of gravity when a six-g turn is like trying to keep your eye on the fly in the room with the refrigerator on your chest. G suits with inflatable bladders squeeze your lower body to equalize, and the pressure on the lungs is like sucking air from a vacuum. Cockpit tapes of my weapons officer sound like Camille on speed. You think you have a fix on this kind of aggression? You think you know what we're about?

We do high-level crisscrossing over targets, probables, background colors. AWACS and everyone else is helping out, telling us what's over the next horizon. Our information is better than anyone else's. Our information is topflight. Our information is provided in excess. We work toward a surprise-free environment. Surprises are for someone else. Surprises are for the dot in the distance. A mile away is too close, and a mile away is a speck on the canopy. Everyone we know is tracking that dot. That dot's trying to track us. All too soon we're going to come to some sort of understanding.

We arc and slice the upper atmosphere, wingleader off to our right, our wings pulling ice from the slipstream, the sun electric bolts on the titanium. This is no simulation; this is the real thing, the difference between thinking about kissing and kissing. We pull an inverted S, and Deadeye in the seat behind cuts loose with a Sparrow, a nice bowed arc, and that dot with the bad information goes like a flashbulb when the two wakes converge. Smoke fingers spider down the curve of the horizon. We helix around a big trailing piece for as long as it falls. Every day, this is what we want. Once back down on dirt we come out of our cockpits marked by our masks, faces shining. Back home they got it half right. We do this for our country. We do it for ourselves.

Nosferatu

EXTERIORS

Six weeks of exteriors: the Carpathians, the Baltic towns of Wismar, Rostock, and Lübeck, as well as ocean vistas of Heligoland and the Frisian Islands in the North Sea. All shooting, exterior and interior, must be finished by November 1921. We begin here, in Czechoslovakia. Half the company has yet to arrive; those who have are filled with questions. Nothing of course has gone as planned. To add to the confusion there are my daily visits to foreign doctors, to say nothing of the visits of nurses to me. But already the film takes me from the soft anguish of idleness and drives me from any room where I cannot work.

I will not aim at poetry. I will try to build a table. It will be for you to eat at it, criticize it, chop it up for firewood.

On the long train trip here I wrote the first title from Hutter's diary, which will introduce the story: *Nosferatu. Doesn't the name*

*sound like the midnight call of a death bird? Beware of uttering it,
or the pictures of life will turn to pale shadows, nightmares will rise
up from the heart and nourish themselves on your blood. For a long
time I have been meditating on the rise and fall of the Great Death
in my father's town of Wisborg. Here is the story of it: In Wisborg
there lived a man named Hutter with his young wife Ellen.*

Wangenheim, who plays Hutter, has been tiresome since the moment I cast him. At the first production meeting he looks over the room assignments (fourth and top floor: art director Albin Grau, cameraman Fritz Arno Wagner, scenarist Henrik Galeen, and myself) and complains the hotel rooms have been apportioned hierarchically. Everyone looks to me as director to establish authority by quashing this kind of petty revolt. Wangenheim sticks a chin out, and makes a petulant face. He's a left-winger and probably feels isolated in this crew.

There *is* a hierarchy, I tell him. I congratulate him for having noticed. And the arrangement is so our collaboration can continue at any and all hours. Grau, handing out room keys, suggests that he spend less time worrying about accommodations and more worrying about his performance.

An argument ensues as to why I brought my driver, Huber, along; one of those film company spats: unpleasantness tinged with subtextual insinuation. Wangenheim, a womanizer, told Grau on the train here that the Prana company would be better served by a director not of my "propensities." Why, he wants to know now, was there scrimping and saving on one end and unnecessary splurging on the other? Huber, I remind everyone, has Czech in his background and could well prove to be invaluable. The usual sort of grumbling and grumping before the rebel angels retreat, quiescent for now and probable trouble later.

Nosferatu

. . .

The company, like a class of children, never understands: it's not a matter of severity or love; it's a matter of clear discernment, and devotion to the work at hand. Behind my back, they poke fun at my unwillingness to show emotion, even in disagreements. It is simple, simple, simple: by remaining master of myself, I remain master of my company. This is all I need to remember. Without that first mastery, all of my authority is very quickly at an end.

The week before we left, *Der Film* finally announced the founding of the Prana Film GmbH company, with a capital of twenty thousand marks. Two managers were named: Enrico Dieckmann, a merchant in Berlin-Lichterfelde, and Albin Grau, artist/painter in Berlin. The name of the company was explained (the reference is to the Buddhist concept *prana*, "vital breath") and attributed to Grau, who, we were informed, "reflects a great deal on the occult aspects of life." Accompanying the announcement was a list of nine films (!) scheduled for production next year, each illustrated with a drawing of Grau's. At the very bottom in small print we learned that directing Prana's first production, *Nosferatu, a Symphony of Horrors*, would be one F. W. Murnau. "Artistic direction"—apparently a separate category—would be handled by Albin Grau. "Together," the announcement concluded with a wan and affected flourish, "they propose to construct the film on new principles."

For the inn in the Carpathians we're filming in Dolný Kubín. A dismal, crooked little town perched like a tooth on a hill. Father would say, "What kind of work would take you to a place such as this?" I imagine him, when people ask, responding simply: "He's in Slovakia." The castle, Oravský Zámok, is not far from town.

Wagner discovered it months ago and sent me a postcard. It was built on the river Orava in the thirteenth century, high up on a curiously hollowed-out rock. The most elevated part is a watchtower that overhangs the Orava more than one hundred meters. The watchtower, shot against the light, will form the final image of the shadow of the vampire passing from the earth.

Tomorrow we begin shooting on the dilapidated terrace, with Wangenheim, who so far has had only useless ideas as to his portrayal of Hutter. Still awake. This preparation, so much of my life since December: how much does it avail me now?

We start with Hutter's discovering the marks on his neck, writing Ellen. It will be in bright sunlight, against a ruined stone wall. We must make certain the vines have been cleared from the battlement. We must counter excess shadow with lamps. We must be ready should the weather not cooperate. If the terrace scene comes off we'll go to Hutter's search for the coffin. After the arch I'll pass in and do the stairway, to the right of where he sees the bolted door leading down. . . .

Sleepless, I wander the corridors. In the stillness, murmurs and flickering light under Grau's door. I knock softly, and enter. Grau and Galeen are sitting cross-legged around a guttering candle. Shadows bend around the recesses of the room. Still uninvited, I sit. We share a bottle of Hungarian wine. We hear mice gnawing at the walls' interior. Grau repeats his story of the old peasant with whom he was billeted in the Army. The peasant was convinced that his father, who died without receiving the sacraments, haunted the village in the form of a vampire. He showed Grau an official document about a man named Morowitch exhumed in Progatza in 1884. The body showed no signs of decomposition, and the teeth were strangely long and sharp, and protruded from the mouth. The man was proclaimed undead, known in Serbia as the Nosferatu. Grau an ardent spiritualist. His next project, he's told me, will be something called *Höllenträume: Dreams of Hell.*

Galeen, too, has a vampire story, from a cousin who served in Austria-Hungary. Galeen is always slightly off-putting, watchful and disquieting. He has a round, bulbous face, with lank brown hair and beautiful skin and an odd and pointless smile. He is only twenty-nine, four years younger than Grau and myself, and was born in Berlin. He tells us the following, in his smooth voice: After it had been reported in a nearby village that a vampire had killed three men by sucking their blood, his cousin was, by high decree of the local Honorable Supreme Command, sent there to investigate, along with two subordinate medical officers. This is the story they were told: Only days after the funeral of a girl by the name of Stana, eighteen years old, who had died in childbirth two weeks previous, and who had announced in a fever before her death that she had painted herself with the blood of a vampire, the family caught sight of the deceased sitting before the front steps of her house. The dead girl repeatedly appeared afterwards at night in the street, and knocked on doors. Children sickened and died. She had relations with an addled widower. When at night, like a trail of fog, she would leave a farm, she left a dead man in her wake. Galeen's cousin and the other officers were taken the afternoon they arrived to the graveyard to open and examine the suspicious grave. When they exhumed the girl, she was whole and intact with blood flowing from her nose, mouth, and ears. When the girl's mother saw her, she spat and said, "You are to disappear; don't get up again and don't move!" At those words tears flowed from the corpse's eyes. Upon seeing that, the villagers pulled her out of the grave, cut her into pieces, and tied them with cloth. The cloth they threw on a thornbush which they set on fire. Whereupon a strong wind arose and blew after them, howling, all the way back to the village.

The first day is overcast. It's always a question of the intensity of the light. Wagner's assistants test it with orange filter glasses. We wait. At eleven I announce we'll set up the close-ups; for those we don't need sunlight. No sooner are we ready than the sun is out. We go on, but now Wangenheim and Greta are squinting; Wagner and his assistants have to screen with canvas the very sun we've been waiting for all day, fake the half-light we've suffered through to this point. Flies circle everywhere. The wind shakes a background I want still. The camera develops a perceptible tremor. Wangenheim abominable.

Day two: more camera troubles. Drove off at nine o'clock. Spectacular trip. Stopped at a wine tavern, and then continued off the main road to show Huber the avenue of Caspar David Friedrich trees that Grau showed me earlier. Pointed out to him as well the pitched waterfall Hutter can see from his room in the castle the night of the greatest danger. Every time I view the place it's a revelation. Huber astounded. The grottoes and clefts and riot of overhanging branches enclosed us with the sound and force of the cataract. We could see movement flitting above in the narrow and overgrown cliff faces. We were in a world where all was wonder, delicate and secret, and besides which all our clutter looks like a farce in bad taste. On the way home by a different route I was talking to Huber about the second inn where Hutter is warned against proceeding to the castle, and round a bend all at one glance I recognized, down to the smallest detail, the exact setting I had resigned myself to having to build. Here were the half-moon windows for Hutter's view of the frightened horses, the old shutters with the carved hex signs, the doors and boxed-in bed, the stone well, the apples piled in an oaken bucket, everything! The interiors as good as the exteriors, with this quality of the luminous strangeness of the ordinary shining through the walls. . . .

Huber too is fascinated with the lore of vampires. He reads a number of Slavic languages and has helped with the forbidding and disintegrating texts Galeen has pulled from the local libraries. We never have enough background material, and what we have always feels too vague. At night, sitting on my bed in my room, Huber reports, his voice transforming the softest consonants into sounds that make my neck ache with desire: Among the Slavs it's reported that one may strew ashes or salt around headstones in a cemetery to determine, by looking for footprints later, if any of the bodies are leaving their graves at night. If a grave is sunk in, if a cross has tipped, the deceased is a vampire. Often there is visible a hole in the grave from which the vampire emerges. And the Gypsies believe that if dogs are barking, there are no vampires in the village, but if dogs are silent, then the vampire has come.

One of Wagner's assistants is spending this week filming the light at dawn (real) on the castle gates (constructed), opening on a fade every morning until *Morgengrau* becomes *Morgengrauen:* "morning's dawn" becomes "morning horror." I have a very specific effect in mind, and think this stock can capture it. Then he'll be sent home to film, for the long shots of the Bremen house of the vampire, the dilapidated salt storehouses of Lübeck. All those empty window-sockets, so that they seem almost more emptiness than brickwork, with an uncanny anthropomorphic quality.

. . .

Talking with Wagner to clarify some ideas: the shot is not a painting, dependent only upon the expressive content of its static
composition; it's also a space negotiable in every way, open to
every sort of intrusion and transformation, inviting the most un-
predictable courses. I must understand the process by which the
mood and tone of such spaces can change. If the question becomes not only What is the image? but How does it change? we
can exploit precisely that connection between film and dream;
the spaces will shift with the logic and fluidity of the dreamstate.
The geography of the film must be evocative yet elusive; the vampire's castle, the wilderness, the various journeys should be concrete in their tone and unmappable in their contours. Reality,
but with fantasy; they must dovetail.

Wagner agreed, and offered this, as well: in Rubens's engrav-
ing of the sheep, which Goethe showed to Eckermann, the
shadow is on the same side as the sun.

Second full production meeting tonight. All of us—Wagner,
Grau, Huber, Galeen, myself, Max Schreck, who will be playing
the Nosferatu—sitting around in my room. Some wine and
sausage. Talking about the sources of horror. Grau claims our
new art has an advantage over literature, because the image can
be clear and concrete even as it remains inconceivable. And that
is the paradox that causes the hair on the back of our necks to
rise. Wagner adds that what people look for in film is a way to
load their imagination with strong images, and the fact that these
images are silent is a supplementary attraction; they're silent like
dreams. I think he's right, for as Hofmannsthal points out, we
have only apparently forgotten our dreams; in fact there's not a
single dream that, reawakened, does not begin to stir: the dark
corner, the breath of air, the face of an animal, the glide of an un-

familiar gait, all of it makes the presence of dreams perceptible. The blackness below the stairs to the cellar, the barrel filled with rainwater in the courtyard, the door to the granary, the door to the loft, the neighbor's door through which the beautiful woman casts into the dark and palpitating depths of the child's heart an unexpected thrill of desire . . .

We fall silent, passing the wine. Huber says it is like traveling through the air in the company of Asmodeus, the demon who raised roofs and laid bare all secrets.

Wagner says he imagines a future film which will be nothing on screen but beautiful creatures and transparent gestures, looks in which the entire soul is read.

Galeen has been listening to all of this, his elbow on the arm of his chair, his palm cupping his round face. It's necessary, he says, to correct the dictionaries. The majority of terms today no longer correspond to the ideas whose image they were intended to provide. Are love, friendship, heart, and soul still the same concepts they were when the ancient dictionaries were composed? What do the old "fantastic" worlds of Grimm, Hoffmann, or Poe represent for us today? Let us, he says, consider them with modern eyes: they remain a source of inspiration, nothing more; for what we have daily before us goes beyond even Jules Verne. Douglas Fairbanks's flying carpet already bores today's young; they sniff out special effects and look for the artifice that made them possible. We are no longer astonished by the technically unheard-of. We are surprised on those days the newspaper does not trumpet new breakthroughs. So we look for the fantastic within ourselves. We notice the child or the dog who walks to the mirror, caught by the miracle of this doubled face. We wonder: If this second self, the Other, were to come out of the mirror's frame? . . .

Empty wine bottles are pyramided on their sides against the

wall like artillery rounds. Grau, slightly drunk, eyes Huber. There has been more tension as to Huber's presence on the payroll. Prana as a new production company according to Grau can afford little extravagance. In Berlin we quarreled about it while we stalked around the station platform with the company's train tickets in our hands. Grau is ambitious, given to wild statements intended to cow the listener, and Prana, which is really a creation of his will and rhetoric, is all he has. I told him Huber was indispensable to helping me think, and dream, and that he seemed important to the project in ways I could not yet articulate. Grau says he's accepted my explanation. Even so, Huber remains uncomfortable in his presence.

Wagner peers into an empty bottle. Grau is slumped to the floor, his head against the door of a low cupboard. Galeen still has his chin in his hands. Only Schreck seems unaffected by the wine, looking each of us over in turn.

The meeting has petered out. To finish we toast our enterprise: Grau the good fortune of the company, Galeen the spirits around us who work with us, Schreck the undead, Wagner the new cameras ordered from Berlin, and myself my young collaborator Huber, whose modesty causes him to doubt his contribution to my work. There is a silence. Huber's eyes shy from mine. Afterwards, he is the last to leave. He stands with his back to me, rummaging in the mess for his coat. I come closer, still without touching him, and he eludes my hand nimbly, like a beautiful animal. I'm reminded of a title from *Phantom*: *She stands in front of him, still drawing back but trying to attract him to her.*

I have always been a fugitive and a vagabond. For a thousand years none of our family has remained anywhere without growing uneasy, without being seized by wanderlust. I am at home in no house and in no country.

Nosferatu

The Murnaus have always been aloof, have always designed their own worlds. Though my father ran his uncle's textile business and was related to the best families in town, he went his own way, bought a magnificent estate at Wilhelmshöhe, with land, hunting, a carriage, and a horse. We children were delighted. The garden had everything we could wish for—a grotto, a ruin, a secret pond, a giant stone, a trapeze. It was a miniature paradise.

Even then he was frightened for me: the way I read every book that came into the house; the way I got too close to special friends. During holidays he would take thick volumes out of my hands and have me contemplate nature instead. He was mortified by my theatrical activities.

Bernhard was the first to visit me in Berlin. That first night I joked with him about Father letting his youngest son out in Sodom with the notorious Wilhelm, and he told me he'd been strictly forbidden to move in certain of my "circles." When by accident we met Huber on the Spichernstrasse, Bernhard took his leave, and did not meet me the next morning as planned.

I am both my father and Something Else, and remain mute before the ongoing miracle of the coexistence of the two.

Talked with Schreck about the Nosferatu. Schreck is a very strange man: narrow-shouldered, peculiarly stiff and clumsy, strikingly ugly without any makeup. At lunch he knocked over his water glass with a wooden sweep of his arm and then simply watched it, glared at me and then the water as it ran across the table. Intensely private, yet he's begun to follow me around, trying to absorb as much as he can. His performance is absolutely crucial. He has had very little experience but when I saw him bending without pleasure over a child on the Kurfürstendamm I knew he was the Nosferatu. I have begun talking with him about his role the only way I know how: trying to articulate the sources of my own obsessions. His silences seem equal parts hostility and understanding.

I talked of the vampire's parasitism — "you must die if I am to live." I talked of the loathsomeness and the dread of his allure. I talked of the way the terrible inhumanness of him, the nightmarish repulsiveness, should move easily among the bourgeois naturalism of the costumes and acting styles of the rest of the cast — the way everyone must see him as *not out of the ordinary.*

More midnight work with Huber on Galeen's script while the rest of the company sleeps. The hotel is silent. In the distance someone is drawing a wagon up the road.

Huber reports quietly on his readings; lays out on the bed charcoal drawings of amulets and charms, diabolic designs. The vampire, he believes, first appears in a Serbian manuscript of the thirteenth century in which a *vuklodlak* is described as a creature which devours the sun and the moon while chasing clouds. Among the contemporary Slavs, *vampir* and *vuklodlak* (literally, "wolf's hair") are synonymous. He reads aloud from a fragment of fifteenth-century Turkish apocrypha: "The Force of Destruction is always near man and follows him like his shadow. For this reason man must always be restored. This restoration occurs in various forms: through the tears of the Force of Creation, i.e., water (bathing and washing); through the breath of the Force of Creation, i.e., air (ventilation of the house, and living outside); and through meeting every morning the first life-giving rays of the Force of Creation (which are sent from the sun)."

We talk until the sky pales, trading ideas, building together an artifice superior to the work of either of our imaginations alone. We construct a new scene for Hutter's arrival: Distant mountains. Vratna Pass. In the background the fantastic castle of the Nosferatu in the evening light. A steep road leading straight up into the sky. Hutter abandoned by his coach. Something comes racing down—a carriage? A phantasm? It moves with unearthly speed and disappears behind a groundswell. Out of nowhere, reappears. Stops dead. Two black horses, their legs invisible, covered by black funeral cloth. Their eyes like pointed stars. Steam from their mouths. The coachman, whose face we cannot see. Hutter inside. Carriage drives at top speed through a *white* forest! (We'll use meters of negative, like "the land the sun travels through at night" so feared in ancient Egypt.)

The courtyard. The carriage at a halt. Almost in a faint, Hutter climbs down. As if in a whirlpool, the carriage circles round him and disappears. Then, very slowly the two wings of the gate open up. . . .

Six days of shooting. The camera still trembles. The new one sent from Berlin is worse than the old one. I let them develop the bad takes just in case the camera's performed some miracle of its own. Yet some scenes come off beautifully. The scene of the panicking horses Hutter sees from the window of the inn: on a grassy slope, the ground falling away toward the back. Night mists creep up the valley. The horses raise their heads as if frightened and, scattering, gallop away. The white horse spun and shook perfectly, which he refused to do yesterday. The camera just got it. And one, after hours of work, *backed out* of the frame! The effect was marvelous. Even Wagner, for all his exhaustion, was excited by how it will look. The possibility of other people's fatigue never occurs to me.

I must avoid a certain kind of coldness that results from the way I work. It would be fatal.

. . .

Huber gone to Berlin for a few days for what he calls "personal matters." He seems more obtuse about my feelings than most others around here: Grau, Galeen, Greta Schroeder, who seems genuinely to wish me well. Clumsy life going about its stupid work: even when we want to reveal ourselves we're so poor at it that we spend most of our time in self-concealment one way or the other. My experience of him is discontinuous, my attention uneven, my judgment and understanding uncertain.

We viewed a short projection last night. The coach arriving at the inn. Wangenheim crossing the little bridge to the "land of the phantoms." It's irritating to see so little, because the true rhythms will be produced only in the cutting. Can't find the take of the white horse turning with its balked jumpiness, and there's no trace of it on the labels. Awful if that shot lost.

With some of the vistas Wagner hasn't enough courage. He compromises and won't take a bold enough line. The result is a softness to his work that I must overcome. It's all too "beautiful." Whereas I want something more harsh to contrast with the beauty, a starkness and awed sweep. . . .

Grau has done a marvelous job turning what is innate in Schreck into the Nosferatu. His makeup (I must show his hands today) will take three hours.

Endless discoveries. Water from a spring so pure the animals take the trough to be empty. The play of shadow off it in twilight like the marble ceilings of seaside hotels. Grau, in his other hat as producer, overseeing for his beloved Prana, complains that we continue to fall behind our shooting schedule. But what shots! Today an open cart-shed full of rakes, curved scythes, a gray spider on a backlit orb-web, broken sunlight and isinglass. And Wagner's work on this, viewed each night, is breathtaking: in clarity, in richness of detail, in contour. One can find that same soft brilliance in certain kinds of silver polished with skins.

Huber left this note with an idea, for Heligoland: *Ellen waiting for Hutter's return at a seaside graveyard—stark crosses at oblique and neglected attitudes on the dune, with the sea beyond.* A wonderful idea: The natural world enlisted and compromised by the Nosferatu. The natural world operating under the shadow of the supernatural. Enormous tranquillity in the context of unease and dread: for whom is she waiting?

I mention the idea to Grau, without telling him where it originated. An excited discussion grows out of our enthusiasm. Endless polarities—west and east, good and evil, civilization and wilderness, reason and passion, with the contested terrain in every case the body of the woman. But the obsession is not with the oppositions as much as the hypothetical areas between them—with the possibility that they are not such oppositions. Hence the insistence upon, and dread concerning, the connections between Hutter and the Nosferatu, Ellen and the Nosferatu.

Huber back. Lunched with him and Galeen and Greta in Poczamok. Bathed in the river. Raspberries!

Huber brought with him an article reprinted from the *Literarische Welt:* "Murnau has become a new kind of being who thinks directly in photographs. Murnau is a kind of modern centaur: he and the camera are joined together to form a single body." And then this: "Murnau teaches us to *see* the modern film; others will teach us to *feel* it."

. . .

The headaches back. The doctors unhappy with my kidneys. Great pain while urinating. The crew sits about and waits. There are times when I am ashamed of their confidence. What have I achieved so far?

A single day left to do scenes that should take three or four, which is always the way the schedules work out. Wagner points out that for the negative footage the vampire's carriage must be painted *white*, so that it will remain black. In the same way, Schreck must be clothed in white. Multiple disasters and new ideas make the last days on location always a nightmare of clumsiness. Everyone falls over everyone else while the light slowly disappears. Four of us splash paint over the carriage in a fever. Grau fashions a white cloak out of a bedsheet. Eleven in the morning becomes five in the afternoon.

That night I dreamed of my father, the last time I saw him: on the platform of the Berlin railway station, standing amid the depressed and nondescript lower-middle-class passengers. I was leaning out the window of the train. For a moment we looked at each other; then the train moved off and he disappeared among the crowd. Then I was in a dead woman's apartment, gazing at the remains of an unappetizing meal, the head and bones of some smoked fish. A sort of ghost meal.

I lay awake afterwards, and scribbled down an idea for a general shot: Hutter looks around the room which seems to him utterly changed. The damp wallpaper, the stains on the floor, the rough furniture, the depressing well of the courtyard beyond. All these things exude a rank physicality, a bleak hostility, a hostility directed at him.

INTERIORS

The interiors have all been built by Grau and his assistants at the Jofa studios at Berlin-Johannisthal. A hard place to get used to — a huge, dirigible-hangar sort of place, with its exposed steel girders and glass high above us, and the sound harsh and prone to echo. Today we checked the dining hall of the castle for the first time. A little arrangement, like a child's playhouse, erected in the middle of this vast space. Grau enraged by the way his sketches had been realized. He ranted, upbraided, drew new versions in the air, and tore down flats, while I stood by, amazed by his talent and passion. At times this is more his production than mine, and he is the glue, in the face of my weakness, that holds everything together.

He disagreed with me about the next set, the layout of the great hall. He complained the scenic space gave the impression of being cut off by accident. I told him, while the company waited for us to settle this, that the compositions I create are intended to seem part of a larger, organic effect; he said no, no, no, banging a table so that a plate jumped: the artistic decor ought to be the perfect composition at the center of which the action takes place.

Wagner mediated, suggesting we were not so far apart in our desires as we thought. I suggested a compromise: we do it my way. Grau left.

Wagner's steadiness is invaluable. I work beautifully with him, usually by anticipating him. I show him an inferior composition; he looks despondently at it; then gets excited, begins fiddling, and in a few minutes produces exactly what we need.

When Grau returns the three of us walk the set. I eliminate the chairs (too light and too modern), allow the fireplace (which doesn't work). Wagner shows us where he wants the second camera. We make fun of his precision. Grau gets onto his hands and knees with a slide rule, and I shout "Closer! Farther! Closer!" while he moves it incrementally this way and that. Huber watches us from a distance and tells me later we seemed like a family he'd never be a part of.

Outside the studio we wait irritably for taxis. It's raining. Schreck leans against a wall in the darkness, arms folded. He has no hat. Grau is staying at a nearby hotel; Huber and I are going back to town. Schreck asks, out of the darkness, what we think a vampire is. Huber says: Corpses who during their lifetime had been sorcerers, werewolves, people excommunicated by the Church, excommunicated from their lives—suicides, drunkards, heretics, apostates, and those cursed by their parents. Grau, after a pause, looks at me and says: Demons who dwell in the corpses of men, to instruct them in vice, and lead them to wickedness.

The shooting begins and the wolfhound that was Galeen's idea refuses to film. He takes his place all right but leaves as soon as the cameras begin to roll and returns when they're finished. We attempt the simple scene of Wangenheim in his room in the castle, a tiny whitewashed room with sharp angles and a huge, crib-like bed in the period style. He is to read from the Book of Vampires (*"THE NOSFERATU. From the bloody sins of mankind a creature will be born . . ."*) and go to the window, throwing it open to look into the starless night, while beyond his door in the depths of the castle the horror gathers. He swaggers through it, ruining everything. Multiple takes, two or three quiet conversations with him. The film is nearly always finished before one's had the time to get the actors to forget the bad habit of "giving a performance."

Then, through the viewfinder, everything was too washed out.

I begged Wagner to get more contrast into the shot, so we set about dramatizing the light, hanging screens to define the space and to create shadows on the far walls. Then Wangenheim began botching the simple actions, dropping the book, catching his foot in the bedclothes. I hid myself, thinking him more likely to manage it with me not around. At last he made it without disaster to the window, but then it was Wagner's turn: the camera caught on its cable and didn't pan. Grau could stand it no longer, and left. We broke for five minutes and did it once more, with only an hour of time left, and miraculously, everything worked. Everyone relaxed. The scene fell together and even a cat wandered through as if it were at home.

At the end of each day, everything but the sets themselves dismantled and stowed away out of sight. The rights to *Dracula* have never been purchased, and Grau has begun receiving a series of inquisitive letters from solicitors representing Bram Stoker's wife.

Talked to Grau about Wangenheim's costume. Colors offer different sensibilities to light, even in our art of black and white. For the scenes in the castle, Wangenheim should have a blue waistcoat. This is not superstitious or fetishistic; it has to do with the particular value of gray that blue will provide.

Also: first day for Ruth Landshoff, who plays Ellen's sister. The daughter of the shipowner, not even a professional actress, but someone I noticed months ago in the Grunewald, on her way to school. Beautiful and refined, she reminded me of a picture by Kaulbach, and I went to great lengths to meet her mother and ask permission for her to take part in the film during her holidays. I am irresistibly drawn to the idea of *this* woman in my film, in this infernal vision of swarming rats, of pestilential boats, of men who suck blood, of dark vaults, of black carriages pulled by phantom horses. . . .

During a half day's shooting she stands beside me, not sure where else to go. Wangenheim flirts with her. Wagner and I are filming Ellen's sleep connection to the vampire. The only sounds are the turning of the camera and Wangenheim's whispering. It's customary to build sets while shooting's going on, and usually there's a crowd of people standing nearby giving orders at the tops of their voices. But I work in silence, the silence of the film itself. A journalist from my parents' hometown compared work on my set to a "memorial service," presided over by "a tall thin gentleman in his white work coat, standing a bit out of the way, issuing directions in a very low voice."

I don't understand how it is that this generation has not seen the rise of a true poet of film. For all the arts, one is able to cite great masters born to understand them exceptionally. There should come geniuses of the screen who know instinctively what it alone among the arts has the power to do. At the moment we found our stories on novels, stage plays, etc. In the future, we will think film and dream film.

Wagner took me aside with doubts about Wangenheim's performance. He said Wangenheim's aggressive terror inhibited his own. The hero, presented to us as bold/hardy/audacious/daring/venturesome and plucky, suddenly passes from all that to convulsive terror? I agreed, and thanked him, and reminded him it was far too late to replace Wangenheim. It was not what I needed to hear.

For the vampire's arrival: lack of movement makes the eye impatient. *Use those impatiences.*

. . .

Filmed Granach, as Knock, the house agent under the sway of the Nosferatu. A relief working with an old friend. During breaks he told the crew how as students in Reinhardt's theater school in Berlin we'd lie on the floor of the stage box to hear and see him working with actors (he allowed no one to view his rehearsals). The scene came off perfectly. Granach reading the cabalistic letter sent him by the vampire seems dropped in from another world, his spindly hunchbacked figure shifting and jerking, his ugly smile making sense of the strange symbols. A last touch was all his: raising his head, upon finishing, as if greeting the evil. Wonderfully disturbing sense of the diabolism closer to home. The happy accidents of art. As the Austrians say, Es ist passiert— It just happened like that.

Reminder to the labs: the lettering of the titles should be lanky and tortuous, like that of *Caligari*. The background, a poisonous green. A tooth is giving me great pain.

Huber related to me this dream, a dream that he was Ellen, in the film: "I went up to the bedroom before my husband. As I reached the side of the bed I heard the fluttering of a bird. The air was disturbed; it vibrated. I did not light the lamp. I did not draw the curtain. The streetlight across the way provided the only light. I could not keep awake. In the park nearby the wind moved the trees. It was as if I had been chloroformed."

He continues to provide me with information on the lore of the vampire. Alone in my room, unable to sleep, I go over, in his handwriting, the last three stages of the etymological history of the word: the Old Church Slavonic for "fugitive," the early Common Slavic for "the one who drinks in," and the later Slavic for "neighbor."

. . .

First interior shooting of Schreck as the Nosferatu. Made up, he wanders the dining hall set in preparation, and the stonework, windows, and doors come to life. It's we, in our modern clothes, who look like intruders, ridiculous ghosts. The scene of his dinner with Hutter: The hall through the camera appearing to have gigantic dimensions. In the center a massive Renaissance table. In the distance the huge fireplace. The Nosferatu reading Hutter's letter of introduction: sharp ratlike teeth over the lower lip. Over the top margin of the letter his eyes, as he hears the clock strike midnight. A snake hypnotizing its victim. Wangenheim smart enough to stop acting as the drama reaches its height, understanding the audience will have already reached the required degree of tension. Afterwards some executives from Prana, friends of Grau's, in for lunch. A strange meal. Schreck, still made up as the Nosferatu, set his teeth on the table like part of the place setting while he ate his soup.

The pace picks up. It must. One set is struck, the other built in its place, while Grau and Galeen and I confer with the actors for the day's next scene. More kidney trouble has thrown us a week behind, and Grau called me at the Bühlershöh sanatorium to remind me that the rest of the shooting must be finished in four weeks, by November 1; that some sets I'd asked them to save had already been struck; and that I must work more sensibly to avoid unnecessary takes. Film stock already costs thirty marks a meter, and there might not be any more forthcoming, for even with the help of the big banks inflation is making it impossible to raise money.

Twelve-hour shooting days. Many of us are fighting artificial sunstroke, caused by the arcs. Crew members rub raw grated potato on their faces to combat the burn. Nosferatu greeting Hutter, emerging from the darkness of the castle archway. Wagner suggests we use magnesium flares with the arcs to increase the effect of moonlight. Take after take. Schreck sweats and suffers under his makeup, and his forehead looks as if it's been varnished.

Everyone beginning to think about future commitments: Granach going back on stage; Grau soon to begin scouting exteriors for Prana's next film. Wagner working with Lang. Galeen to direct his own *Stadt in Sicht.* We're all progressively losing the sense that we're held within the same dream; each of us is beginning to wake up.

My trouble is naïveté. What I should do is overnumber the shots so that as we progress the script girl could note increasing numbers accomplished each day, and Grau and his production company would be steadily mollified.

Tensions continue with Grau over the schedule, our plans for the film, everything. As we get closer to the end more and more of his energy goes into promotion and distribution, which is necessary but seems to me premature and wrong. A woman journalist interviews him for *Der Film* and a week later I'm subjected to the following: "As always, each scene is given over to the director only when ready to be filmed; beforehand the artistic director has prepared it down to the smallest details according to psychological and pictorial principles, and has sketched it out on paper. Each gesture, each costume (the era of 1840 approximately), each movement has been laid out with scientific rigor and calculated to produce a specific effect upon the spectator."

The publicity material he's prepared has reached a tone that verges on provocation. Part of one of his handouts:

Nosferatu was there. In the streets. Mongrels howled it. Babies cried it. Crooked branches traced its letters in the earth. The wind swept the word and carried it away, and dead leaves from the trees read "Nosferatu." The word invaded everything. One could see it along walls, above streetlamps, in the eyes of those late to bed. It fastened to ganglia and sounded in bones: "Nosferatu." It clamored. It uttered cries like rats in a coffin. Maidens whispered it in their sleep. Above them in the darkness it was livid and ghastly pale, leaden and yellow, full of sulphur and fatal breath. And you? Do you still feel nothing? Nos-fer-a-tu—Nosferatu—beware.

Shot by shot I know my way through. I will not give in until I have what I want. But every morning there we are again on the set, with its dismal fraudulence, flapping wall, plaster gargoyles. Again I'll get worked up, pull my hair, go back to my room, start all over again.

Determined to do ten shots today, despite Wagner's pace, Grau's complaints, and the arcs, which keep fusing. Horrible quarrel. Wagner's taken to calling me the Schoolmaster.

Took Huber to dinner last night at the Goldener Hirsch. He's stayed away from me for days, and I've been too exhausted and busy to do anything but register my disappointment. I'm determined to find out how much is innocence and how much is coyness. This meeting arranged awkwardly, days in advance. While we were being seated, Wangenheim wandered by. It's as though I'm living in a Feydeau farce. Huber seemed frightened, uneasy; I was exhausted and short-tempered. A bad start.

The first stalking of Hutter. Huddled discussions with Wangenheim beforehand. The thing that matters is not what the actors show me but what they hide from me. Above all: *what they do not suspect is in them.* I cite for him the Baroness in *Schloss Vogelöd,* who, after her husband fends off her kiss and announces his renunciation of everything worldly, whispers distractedly to herself, *"I am longing for evil—seeing evil—wanting evil."*

We begin. The set deathly quiet. Hutter in his room in the castle, huddled behind the door. He opens it a crack. View deep into dining hall. By the fireplace the Nosferatu, motionless, arms down, confrontationally stark against the background. Horrible lack of movement. Hutter supports himself on the doorpost. Terrible realizations dawning. Shut the door, shut it quickly! No bolt. No lock. He rushes to the window. (View of the forest at night: undergrowth; wolves raising their heads, howling.) The contrast between Hutter's movements and the Nosferatu's: frenzied panic vs. the terrible evenness of the advance. Hutter on his knees by the side of the bed. Stares at the door, which opens to half its width; opens fully. Superimpositions of progressively closer shots of the vampire, producing movement without movement, the figure swelling within the frame, the mechanism of nightmare. Wagner has the genius idea of having the figure penetrate a powerful light emanating from the side just as he enters the doorway. Four days of work.

Two weeks left. Hardly eating. That same woman journalist from *Der Film* told me today my face was like "two profiles stuck together." Ellen's room, her decision to sacrifice herself, the final approach of the vampire all still left. Two days of work on Ellen reading the Book of Vampires, until my temples are throbbing, my cheeks burning, my whole frame shivering. A few hours in my room drinking hot soup. Realizing mistakes I made by plunging on at such a pace; but besides the lack of time, I feel myself fighting to prevent any kind of indecision at this point from demoralizing the unit.

My headaches worse. My kidneys breaking down. Berliners

are tactless and cruel. On a bus yesterday a young lieutenant seated me with a flourish. The spectacle of this disintegrating thirty-three-year-old seems to make people laugh.

Take after take of Ellen at the window, seeing the Nosferatu. Greta not up to it. Wagner has the inhumanity of all cameramen; he calibrates the lights at his own pace without noticing that Greta all that time is swaying on her feet. Grau looks on, his arms folded. The nerve storm finally breaks and she collapses. Wangenheim comforts her while we wait. The shooting goes far into the night.

Disaster at home. Received word that Sandri, my handsome Malay servant at the house in Grunewald, ran amok and killed a chambermaid in my absence. The police had to break down part of the house to get at him. Grau considers it a publicity disaster; has spent days making calls to try and control the story's release.

Little sleep; endless, crushing headaches. Granite pieces breaking behind my eyes. Cold sweat, palpitations, exhaustion. A full day without working at all. Grau in a frenzy of rage and despair over this preview, in a Marxist rag: "This occultism, which has victimized thousands of shaken minds since the war, is a strategy mounted by the industrial world to deflect the worker from his own political interests. Today the occult takes the place of religions that no longer attract clients. Workers! On your guard! Don't give your pennies to a spectacle designed to stupefy! Let the phantom 'Nosferatu' be devoured by his own rats!"

Grau's response? Ever more publicity. Prana has now spent more on publicity than on the film itself. It seems clearer and clearer to me that the whole enterprise, beyond this film, is an enormous bluff. Where is that publicity money to come from? Grau, ever the fast talker, says "the Otto Riede Bank," but Wagner has told me that this bank does not exist, and that Otto Riede is a simple employee. Yet the madness goes on. Grau plans a party on the release date: Saturday, March 4, "Prana's Day." He's secured the marble entry hall of the zoo and commissioned a prologue by Kurt Alexander inspired by the introduction from Goethe's *Faust*. He's hired Elisabeth Grube of the national opera to perform with the ballet troupe. For musical accompaniment there will be the great harmonium *Dominator*, transported to the site at great cost. And all of this, he announces, will be filmed!

Hobbled back to the set this morning accompanied by a nurse. Interrupted by the police, concerning Sandri. Disoriented by the medication and exhaustion and worried all day by an oppressive sense that I'm out of touch with the world. Stagehands stood around in groups as if at union meetings, and eyed me. The whole film seemed moribund. Woke that night from dreams which seemed to move like dirty water forming monstrous waves. Neck hurt.

And then a late-afternoon wait in a pub across the street from the studio. Another problem with the arc lights. Wagner, Huber, and I share wine, bread and butter, minced pork. I confess my fears, my inability to understand what I'm doing, or to go on. Wagner tells me that I alone can do this. And Huber, half distracted, puts his hand to my cheek, there before the entire pub. That easily, his palm brings me a temporary peace. He tells me he's been viewing the footage, and that it's been everything I've hoped for. He is such a mysterious figure, finally: cheerless and sober and intent on something outside my view.

. . .

A few hours' sleep. A breathing spell. The final sequence to be done, the Nosferatu's approach to Ellen. The horror coming slowly, tensed like a predatory animal. A new idea, necessitating a new set at this late date by Grau: nothing but the shadow of Nosferatu on the wall of the stairs, mounting with dreadful slowness, then more quickly, an awful quick-footed walk, fingernails dripping, until the gigantic shadow pauses beside the door. The hand and fingers extending elastically along the wall. In the room Ellen shrinks before the monster we still do not see, except for the black shadow of his hand spreading across her white body like ink. She jerks her head down in anticipation of his touch, as her husband had. The shadow fist seizes her heart. In the darkness, on the very side of the frame, obscenely unobtrusive, the Nosferatu feeding.

The shooting done. A week's rest. The unit comes back together one last time to view the rough projection before major cutting begins. Grau, Wagner, Galeen, Wangenheim, Greta, Huber—all of this is now only a memory to them, like a party they found puzzling and absorbing but not pleasant.

Wagner torments me with an article in the *Berliner Tageblatt*, reading for the group: "Of all the film directors, Murnau is the most German. A Westphalian, reserved, severe on himself, severe on others, severe for the cause. Outwardly grim, never envious, always alone, his successes and failures arising from the same source, each of his works complete, authentic, direct, logical, cold, harsh, and absolute, like Gothic art." Much hooting. Grau suggests it sounds like an obituary.

We view what we have. Some pleasures—the opportunity to make fluid human time, normally so painful in its rigidity, to break time up, arrange and rearrange it, our small triumph over

Nosferatu

the inexorable/inevitable. Again struck by the number of times the camera could see what I couldn't feel.

Long stretches of footage so bad no one will comment. Enduring them I begin to tell myself I can still do what I set out to do; yet if there are faults in the work they are mine alone.

In the darkness Huber is comfortable and affectionate. Yet the more promisingly he approaches my goal, the more restrained my passion for him. This sense of never being at home, with anyone, I feel more and more, the older I get.

More footage. My concentration dissipates. I remember living in a series of hotels, when I was very small, before Father bought the estate. One small old hotel in particular, by the sea, a little room full of sun, where you could smell the apples and the waves. I long to film something invested with that kind of emotion.

Someone yawns. Someone shifts in his chair. In the silence of a changeover in reels, I can hear us all—Grau, Huber, Greta— murmuring with pleasure and amusement, and behind the whirring of Wagner cueing up the final leader, we can hear the sound of many voices singing in the garden below: children outside our dark little room, shouting in the sunlight.

Family

Eustace

Against the glass, Sister Emelia's face looked surprising, Biddy realized. Like the blowfish in the encyclopedia. She was yelling something, her eyes wide and her face red, but he couldn't make it out through the double doors. He was scared at first, because she looked like the Flahertys' dog, who always had to be chained up and when he jumped at you was all pink gums and yellow teeth, but that passed. After a while she wasn't funny anymore, either. She yelled something again, shaking the handles on the doors, and he examined her teeth.

Biddy wasn't his real name; it was Eustace Lee, named for some uncle his father always remembered as sharp, as in "Old Eustace Lee was sharp, boy." He didn't like the name Biddy and he didn't like the way strangers would screw up their faces and repeat it when they heard it, but then, he always thought it fit him for some reason, and Eustace Lee was no bargain, either. He never knew where the name came from. His mother claimed it came from his being a little "biddy" baby, but he didn't think even she believed that. It was his from as far back as he could remember. Even Sister Emelia called him Biddy, except when she got mad.

Although later the doctor kept telling everyone how well planned it was, Biddy hadn't decided to do anything until right before recess, and after Sister Emelia had come in for Question Time. He had interrupted Janie Hilgenberg (everybody did), who'd been asking something stupid about when the new bathrooms would be finished anyway, and had asked the same question for the third day in a row about the old drunk and Father Hogan, and the whole class had swallowed together, and it had gotten very quiet. Sister Emelia had put her chalk down and had looked over at him and had gotten red (though not as red as later, against the glass) and then had stood up just as the recess bell rang. Biddy had managed to get outside with the pack. She hadn't followed him out onto the playground. He wasn't fooled. He knew where he was headed after recess and he knew that while yelling had been enough the first two times, it wouldn't be anymore.

—All right now, Biddy, let's try it again. Why'd you lock everybody out?

—Answer the doctor, Biddy.

—Please, Mr. Siebert. It's a little more helpful if you're less of a . . . presence. Biddy?

—C'mon, Biddy. We talked about this. The doctor can't help you unless you want to help yourself. Right?

—Biddy?

—I didn't want to get hit.

—Who was going to hit you?

—Sister Emelia.

—Why was Sister Emelia going to hit you?

—You must've done *some*thing, Biddy. Tell the man.

—Mr. Siebert, this really isn't working out. Would you please take your wife and leave us now? We'll see what we can do on our own.

—Look—you said we could stay the first time.

—I know, but I think we need to be one-on-one here. Please. Walk around. Do some shopping. Come back around three. We'll still be here. Biddy doesn't mind if you go, do you Biddy?

—No.

—Biddy, you're gonna be all right?

—Yeah.

—You gonna remember what we talked about and not waste everybody's time?

—Yeah, you guys go do something.

—We'll be back in a little while. Okay?

—Okay.

—Shut the door all the way. Thanks. Thanks. Okay. Now. Do you want to sit somewhere else? Is that good?

—This is good.

—You ready to talk some more?

—If you want.

—Okay. So. Why was she going to hit you?

—Because I asked about the old drunk again.

—What?

—I asked her about this old drunk, and Father Hogan. It's a long story. It was a stupid question.

—I don't understand.

—It's okay. Nobody does.

—She was going to hit you for asking a question?

—I asked it before. She'd told me to stop asking it. It was like I knew it was going to start trouble.

—How'd you know she was going to hit you?

—She gets this look.

—Has she hit you before?

—Sure. Otherwise why would I be worried?

—And that's when the recess bell rang? What did you do then?

—I went back in. Everybody was out except the two old secretaries in the office and Mrs. Krenning—

—Mrs. Krenning?

—The fifth-grade teacher, so I told the secretaries that Sister Emelia wanted them and Mrs. Krenning that Greg—that's her kid—got hurt on the monkey bars. When they left I locked the doors.

—But . . . let me get this . . . how did you *lock* the doors?

—I had time enough. Sister Emelia left her keys on the desk and I went around and locked them.

—It was that easy? *All* the doors?

—There're only three, not counting the main ones.

—Amazing. And the other sisters didn't have keys?

—Only to the main doors, I think. I remember being early one morning and Sister Theresa saying we had to go around to the front because her keys didn't open the other doors.

—So what about the main doors, then?

—I got Chuck's push broom—he's the janitor—and slid it through the things on the doors. I just jammed it in there.

Sister Emelia hadn't figured out what was going on; nobody had, until they noticed the push broom through the glass and Biddy sitting on the stairs.

He thought, while they pounded and stared in at him, The door's a force field. The planet outside has no air.

He went up to the second floor to follow the nuns' progress

around the building. He could hear the far-off rattle when they tried each door. He stayed near a window with a good view of the street, and some of his classmates found him and stood around below, looking up and pointing. After about twenty minutes his parents came. They were led to the main doors. He stayed where he was. A little bit after that Chuck came and started fooling with the office door in the back, so Biddy went down and stuffed a doorstop under it and then slid the heavy office desks over in front of it end to end until three together just about reached the opposite wall.

He walked up and down the halls before settling into a ground-floor classroom. He hadn't planned on this. However much time he had left was his.

He jumped about three feet when Michael Graham tapped at the window and asked if he could come in, too. There were un-locked windows on both sides of the one Michael was tapping on, and Biddy hurried over, trying to look like nothing was wrong, and locked them, and then ran from the room to check the other windows. Across the hall a seventh grader was trying to get in with a boost from Sister Veronica, and Biddy ran over and tried to pry him loose but he wouldn't let go so Biddy bit his hand and he yelled and fell back onto Sister's head and Biddy shut the window. There were more noises, in the fifth- and first-grade rooms, and he got rid of one quick but the other kept him away by slapping at him with his free hand until he got some erasers from the chalkboard and clapped at the kid's face until his hair was all white and he was choking and gagging and he let go too.

He was coughing himself from the dust, still holding the erasers. He could see the kid he bit outside with the nuns, show-ing off the hand to the other kids.

There was a crash down the hall and he took off, and in the

boys' bathroom there was Sister Theresa, trying to wiggle through the frosted window. She said to him, "Biddy, don't you make it worse, Biddy, don't you *move*," and he took a stack of tiles from the corner from under the new toilet seats and, just out of her reach, slid the frame down tight on her, wedged the tiles in, and left her hanging there yelling his name.

—What do you think of me asking all these questions?

—I ask questions too.

—Uh—that other sister—how did you trap her in the window like that?

—I don't know how she got up that high. Someone must've given her a boost. I got a stack of tiles from the corner and stuck them in the top, you know, like this, so she couldn't move either way.

—Why do you think she tried to climb in, instead of the janitor?

—Chuck's kind of old for things like that.

—But why her, do you think?

—She probably figured she was the skinniest.

—You don't think it was because she was especially worried about you?

—No.

—Is she pretty much your favorite sister?

—I don't know.

—Do you have a favorite sister?

—I guess so.

—Who's your favorite sister?

—She is.

—You know how long she hung there?

—No. I heard her yelling. Then I didn't. I guess they got her when they got me.

—Didn't you worry about her hanging there?

—No. She couldn't move.

—No, I meant . . . why didn't you push her back out, instead of trapping her?

—I didn't think she'd let go.

—Did you try?

—No.

—Why didn't you bite her hand, too?

—I didn't want to. I couldn't.

—Ah. Why not?

—Her fingers are like . . . cold. Like worms. I couldn't.

He sat on the steps of the second-floor landing, watching everyone running around below. His parents were talking to Sister Emelia. The teachers were trying to keep the kids together and quiet on the playground and weren't doing too good a job. Sister Veronica was chasing a kid who'd crossed the street. It was windy and her habit was slowing her up.

He wondered if he'd stay all night. He wondered if he'd find something to eat. He wondered if they'd break something to get at him. Then the nuns all ran down to the street and a big black Oldsmobile pulled up—Father Hogan's car—and he knew he wouldn't be staying all night.

—You never thought that all they'd have to do is get ahold of Father Hogan?

—No. I forgot about him.

—You didn't think all along that he'd come and let them in?

—No. That's a dumb question.

—Why?

—Because. It's dumb.

—Why is it dumb?

—Because! If I knew they'd get back in, why would I lock them out?

—What did you think when he drove up?

—I don't know.

—What did you do?

—I ran down and tried to jam up the last doors.

—And you couldn't.

—There was nothing around, and I heard them coming.

—So what did you do?

—I ran. I ran up to the top. I ran into a room but it was stupid to try and hide and I knew it so I came back out to the stairs.

—Who was the first person you saw?

—Sister Emelia.

He crouched at the top of the stairs, rolling back and forth on the balls of his feet. Sister Emelia came up slowly, one hand gripping the rail. He saw what he should do—what he should've done long ago—sail down those stairs he'd walked down so much. And he was out, arms outstretched, and Sister Emelia's open mouth was rushing up at him and there was a shock, first soft, then hard as they tumbled down the stairs, the loud *ka-thumping* mixing weirdly with Sister Emelia's shrieks. Then they weren't moving, at the bottom, and Sister Emelia's leg was over his chest and everyone was running and shouting.

—Do you remember anything lying there?

—No.

—Do you remember it hurting?

—No. There was a lot of crying and screaming.

—That's because they saw the blood from your head.

—I guess they thought I was dead.

. . .

About seven doctors in a row asked him what happened, and his parents kept asking, too. He got impatient with the question. Sister Veronica had seen what had happened, along with everybody behind her on the stairs. They asked if he liked the food. They asked if he was warm enough. They played with his feet and asked if he could feel it. They asked if he wanted anything to read or anything from home, and when he couldn't think of anything to say, his mother cried.

— You said something a few sessions ago about an old drunk.
  — Uh-huh.
  — Tell me about the old drunk. Where did you see him?
  — McDonald's.
  — What was special about him? Why'd you notice him?
  — Nothing was special about him.
  — Then why'd you notice him?
  — I don't know. It's stupid.
  — I may not think so.
  — It's stupid.

He didn't like McDonald's any more than his father did. But his mother was refusing to cook again, so there they were. It was empty except for some old men in a booth by the bathrooms. One of the guys had the sleeve torn off his jacket. Biddy's father said, Meeting of the Board, and nodded at them. Biddy watched them until his father told him to stop staring and finish his shake. The one with the missing sleeve had amazing eyes. They locked onto something and then shot over and locked onto something else. He talked like soon he wasn't going to be allowed to talk again, and he had sweated through his shirt in the middle. The other old men were losing interest in him. The booth got into a fight over somebody's fries, and the manager had to go over. Biddy's father shook his head and Biddy felt terrible and wasn't sure why. He didn't finish his shake and when they got up to go his father gave him that look and told him he'd better start eating.

—You mind your parents not being here when we talk?
—No.
—Why not?
—They were sorta a pain, I guess.
—Ah. Why do you feel that way?
—I mean to you.
—Oh. Are they ever a pain to you?
—No.
—Never?
—No.
—Do they understand lots of things, you think?
—No.
—Do they understand most things?
—No.
—Does that bother you?
—No.
—Do you think they try to understand?
—I don't know.

He tried to explain about the old man in the car on the way back, but he couldn't figure it out himself. His father listened for a while and then told him he should've spent more time eating and less trying to make eye contact with the homeless. Some of those guys looked pretty belligerent, his father said. And he was not eating enough, that was problem number one. Mr. Skin and Bones.

Sister Theresa wasn't too interested in the old man either. The more Biddy thought about it the more he figured somebody should know, somebody should help. What bothered him was that *he* didn't want to help. So he went to Sister Theresa. He asked her: Maybe it was crazy, but couldn't Father Hogan be a sort of missionary? Didn't priests want to be missionaries? He recognized the lameness of his good deed: *couldn't someone take care of this for me?* Wasn't there something—it didn't have to be that big—that someone could do?

At the conference with his mother and Sister Theresa he tried to explain that all they had to do was go down there and see the guy, but Sister Theresa kept asking the wrong questions, and his mother cried.

—Why don't you talk about things with your mother?
—Who said I didn't?
—Do you talk about things with your mother?
—No.
—Uh-huh. Why not?
—I don't know. Are we almost finished for today?
—Almost. Do you tell your mother things that happen during the day?
—I don't know.
—Do you tell her what you like and don't like?
—No.
—Why not?
—Because. I don't know. She knows, I guess. We don't fight.

Biddy didn't like Froot Loops. He didn't like the way they got so sweet after a few mouthfuls or how they turned the milk pink. There was a time when he would eat things he didn't like, but he didn't see any reason to anymore. And he didn't like Froot Loops.

So they sat together patiently, Biddy and the Froot Loops, waiting for his mother to give in and throw the dish into the sink, spilling milk and soggy Froot Loops across the counter, and to say again, "And your father yells at me because you're not eating."

He would feel bad when she did, but, after all, Froot Loops were Froot Loops.

—Didn't your mother say you had some pets? A turtle, or something?
   —No.
   —You never had a pet?
   —I had a canary once.
   —Did your parents give it to you?
   —I got it at Woolworth's.
   —What was his name?
   —Nero.
   —Why Nero, do you think?
   —I don't know. I like Roman stuff.
   —So what happened to Nero?
   —My mother gave him away. He was pretty sick, too.
   —Why'd she do that?
   —I didn't take care of him.
   —What didn't you do? Did you not feed him or something?
   —I didn't take care of him.
   —Were you mad at your mother for that?
   —Maybe wherever he went he got better.
   —Do you ever miss him?
   —No.
   —Do you think he ever misses you?
   —I don't think so.
   —Why not?
   —He was a canary.

. . .

He had no idea they'd been waiting three days for him to ask about Sister Emelia. They were mad. His mother said, "Biddy, don't you even care?" in such a way that he was scared that some part of himself he needed for that was missing. The doctor said he was sure it had just slipped his mind, and his mother after talking about it for a while felt better. His father stared at him. He tried to watch TV. He wondered if he should ask about Sister Emelia.

—Let's talk about Sister Emelia. . . . You don't mind, do you?
—No.
—When did you find out she was hurt?
—When they told me.
—Did you feel bad for her?
—I guess.
—You guess?
—I guess.
—Was she your least favorite teacher?
—I guess.
—Why was that?
—She hit people.
—Is that the only reason?
—She yelled a lot. She hit people and she yelled a lot.

He never got as upset as other kids after he got slapped. Michael Graham and Luis were always getting slapped and their mothers were always coming in and getting mad at Sister Emelia sometimes and at Michael and Luis sometimes, and neither did any good. Biddy never thought it would.

He didn't mind the bandages on his head. Everybody in the hospital thought he did and asked about it, but he didn't. For a while he wished they were over his mouth, too. It would look good, nothing showing but his eyes. He wouldn't have to talk, either. Still, the bandages and everything made his mother cry more easily, and she cried a lot before.

After his parents fought nobody talked and that was okay with him. A lot of times after supper his mother would go into the den and turn the TV up and cry. He wasn't big on TV so he would go upstairs. Then the next meal would be quiet, and they'd tell him to stop playing with his food, but they'd only say it once. His mother would cry during meals if it was a bad fight. He tried to eat everything so they wouldn't argue about why he wasn't eating. Mostly he liked breakfast, because he ate breakfast alone.

His mother kept asking if he was excited about going home and he didn't feel like making her cry so he said he was and she seemed better. His father told him he should "go easy" but he didn't really know what that meant. His last night in the hospital when his parents were getting ready to go his mother told him everything was going to be all right, and he knew she was going to start crying again. She started in the hall and he wished the fall had made him deaf instead of breaking his head.

—You looking forward to going back to school tomorrow?
  —I guess.
  —Are you worried about it?
  —I don't know.
  —Are you worried you'll get into trouble again?
  —No.
  —Why not?
  —I won't get into trouble.
  —Why not?
  —I won't.

—This is our last session for a while, Biddy. What do you think? Did we learn anything?

—Mmm.

—Do you feel better?

—Mmm.

—Do you?

—Better.

—Well, if you start to have trouble again, you can come back, right? And we can talk about it, right?

—Mmm.

No one spoke to him except Luis, who wanted the rest of his Yodel. He played kickball out front and everybody got quiet when he came up. He tripled and it was like the sound was turned off. No one looked at him until it was Question Time and Sister Emelia came in with her neck brace. She asked if there were any questions. There weren't.

The Touch of the Dead

I was home from college, I was sitting with my grandmother, and it was night. I had my hands in my lap; she was in a lot of pain. Her foot was twisted under. She'd gone to the bathroom somewhere in the room. She didn't make sense and at times said I was my father. She was telling me about her day or her dreams. She was talking it up now that we were alone. She said, "Chelsea thinks there are tornadoes coming. I went over to the window and Salvatore was outside in the pool."

Chelsea was her cat. Salvatore was my father.

"Salvatore was up to his waist in the pool," my grandmother said.

"This was a dream, I think, Grandma," I told her.

She agreed with that completely. She said, "The sky went black on top and you could see it moving, the sky, and these things started to come down, like whips, alive."

I was there for the most part to find her cat. Something had spooked her cat and it was holed up in one of the heating vents in the living room. My uncle had taken off the grating for some reason, and you could see the cat's eyes way back in there around a turn.

Chelsea had been with my grandmother for fourteen years. My uncle and father had tried to get the cat out with a dish of food, a broom handle, and salad tongs. I was the next resort. I was pretty thin. My grandmother was upset about the cat, and that upset my father and uncle.

She made the drinking motion with her hand. There was a Dixie cup of milk still on her tray. "Who's that?" she said.

"It's me," I told her. "Eddie."

I was taking a break from the cat. My first attempt I'd gotten a shoulder in and scraped the other one pretty bad. I'd torn my shirt and my collar was raggedy.

She said something I didn't get and I had to lean forward. Her teeth weren't in and I missed a lot of what she said.

I cupped my ear. Her knee was raised in front of me and the tumor had swelled it. My mother told me it was like the rest of her was all going into her leg. I leaned forward.

"You're no good for nothing," she said. "You leave me alone."

My forehead got cooler. I wasn't too close to my grandmother, but this was still a shock. In the kitchen a coffee cup clinked and a faucet turned on. It didn't sound like she was talking about the cat. I told her she was talking to Eddie.

"I know who it is," she said, nodding her head. "I know who it is."

"How is she?" my father said. He was in the doorway. "She recognize you?"

"I don't know," I said. I felt like I could tip from the bed so I put my hands out.

"Mama," my father said in his loud voice. "It's Salvatore. How you feel?"

She repeated his name.

My uncle Armond called from the kitchen that she'd been like this since yesterday. Thursday she'd been something. Thursday she'd had the yardstick, was waving it at him. "You get outta here!" she was going. "This is my house!"

My father snorted. I asked him about her hands.

He guessed it was the cortisone. My uncle came in and told us that the doctors thought she had a system like Man o' War's. We should see the pills. He showed us some from a bottle on the dresser, and they were the size of quarters. She couldn't take them, my uncle said. All this from a Dr. Kildare who couldn't bring himself to touch her.

He pointed. We looked where he was pointing. "He stands over there. 'How are we today, Mrs. Spadacinno? Any more pain?'"

"They're all terrible," my mother called. She was still in the living room, poking around the vent. Her idea was a serving fork with tuna fish on it. "They're good at billing."

"Tornadoes," my grandmother said. She looked at us.

My father made his sad noise and put his hand on the back of his neck. He said, "What about tornadoes, Ma? What about them?"

I said, "Does she recognize us?" Every time I'd thought nothing about her, every time she'd been another pain-in-the-ass thing in the day, she'd remembered, and now she was laying it out for all of us to see, the way you lay down rows of cards in solitaire.

"I think she does," my uncle said. He raised his voice. "You recognize Eddie, don't you?" he said. "Eddie's here. Sal's brought Eddie."

My uncle thought I didn't contribute much to the family. I'd heard him ask my father over the phone if I thought I was any different than the rest of the *cavones* who had to make an appearance occasionally.

I was going to college. I'd missed a funeral because of Winter Carnival.

"Eddie," my grandmother said. She didn't smile.

My mother came in, eating the tuna. She asked how my grandmother'd been eating.

She liked the vanilla pudding, my uncle said. He mixed in some maple syrup.

"She's got a sweet tooth," my father said. "You got a sweet tooth, don't you?"

"Hah?" my grandmother said. She shifted around, and brought her cheeks back from her gums.

"You wanta move, Ma?" my uncle said. "You in pain?"

"Lea' me alone," she said.

So we all just sat there. I ended up looking over the stuff on the doily on her dresser. She had a comb and brush, a picture of my father and uncle, and a squatting porcelain kid with a flute. My mother said that that was something that Tony'd gotten her. Tony was my brother, the grandkid she really liked. Tony wasn't here.

"I lived a long life," my grandmother said. Oh, God, I thought.

My uncle told her she had to put her teeth in. He pointed to them.

"What's she saying?" my mother asked.

"She's wondering where Tony is," I said.

"She says she's all right," my uncle said.

"We know you're all right," my father said in his loud voice. He shot me a look. "We wanta help anyway."

"Lea' me alone," she said. She stared out at us.

I was the one everyone expected to be there. Tony was the one everyone wanted to be there. My grandmother sent me fifteen dollars every Christmas. She sent Tony twenty-five. This was because Tony was older. I didn't want to be petty and I didn't want to measure things by money, but I got fifteen and he got twenty-five, every year.

I'm not sure my grandmother had any right to like me.

I told everyone I should go back to the cat. At the vent I knelt down and put both palms on the rug. I looked in. The cat had re-settled itself, and its nails made thin sounds on the metal. While I had my rear in the air my uncle came by and pushed me over with his foot. He asked how things were going.

Economics sounded like a racket to him. He ran a construction company, A. Spadacinno, General Contracting. They did mostly asphalt parking lots and driveways, but they did buildings as well. Tony had worked for him a couple summers; I never had. Tony hadn't gotten along with him. But nearly every interaction between my uncle and me made it clear that not getting along with him was better than never working for him.

I stuck my arm in as far as it would go and eased my head in. The sound of my breathing changed. My fingers stopped about two inches short of the cat and I thought about the serving fork. My uncle talked about the Christmas when my grandmother had been caught at our house by a snowstorm. When I tried to answer, everything echoed and he said he couldn't hear me.

We'd all listened to Jimmy Roselli, *Buona Natale*.

I could hear my father in the room behind him. He said we weren't going to get anywhere with this and for me to come out. My uncle made a crack and they laughed. I jerked my arm farther in and my shoulder popped. My fingertips brushed the cat and it backed in farther around the curve in the vent. I laid there for a minute and then I squeezed out. I scraped my ear, and sat rubbing it, and told them the cat had gone farther in.

My mother came out of my grandmother's room and we got ready to go. Everyone hugged. I went along the wall next to the vent thumping it with my foot until my father told me stop.

In the car he said I could get the bus back up to school tomorrow. There was no sense in my waiting around. The cat would come out on its own.

It didn't. For three days it stayed in there somewhere.

While it was still in there my grandmother died.

My uncle called to tell us. I was still home. Tony was out West somewhere, we thought, around Denver. One of the first things my father tried to do was get through to him. He asked me to keep trying when he couldn't. He was broken up; my mother was with him in their bedroom. I called around to some of the numbers we had. After I dialed I put my finger on the hang-up thing. Sometimes I made like there was no answer. Sometimes I invented conversations.

At the wake I unhooked the velvet cord and sat on the carpeted stairs leading up to the undertaker's home and answered questions as to where my brother was. Sometimes I said, "I have no idea." I resisted saying, "Isn't he here?" A little girl on the top landing brushed the rug with her flat palm and kept an eye on me. She said, "You're on our stairs." I told her it was okay and she said, "Get off of our stairs."

At the wake my father and uncle had to take one of my aunts into the little room for coats and shut the swinging door. She screamed and hiccuped.

In the bathroom I heard one guy I didn't know say that Salvatore's mother had that thing with her leg all those months, you think they ever got her a nurse round the clock? Two brothers, you think between them they ever got her a full-time nurse? Her leg out to there.

The other guy said he heard they were loaded.

I'd made us take two cars, thinking I'd go early. I gave it three hours and then told my father and mother I was hitting the road, and they gave me the nod, go ahead.

I came back an hour later. By then their car was gone. The place was closing. No one saw me walk back in. I hid in the bathroom in one of the stalls. To check for people a guy just stuck his head in and called hello.

I sat on one of the toilets with my feet up. There were mice in the walls. I waited until everyone was gone, and then I came out.

Someone had moved all the flower stands to the back. One bouquet was still swaying. The sash said BELOVED AUNT. The little tag said LILIES: BLACK DRAGONS AND MADONNAS. What did I know about flowers?

The house was dark. It sounded like everyone upstairs was asleep.

The casket was closed and looked like it was floating. It was smooth and dark like a submarine, and when I went closer the room made hostile and shifting noises.

My eyes were still adjusting. Or a fast, dark car, I thought: it looked like a fast, dark car.

I put my hands on the lid panel. I could feel the oil in the polish. The lid was cold and heavy and I opened it. The silk inside made whispery noises.

My grandmother's face had been given this look like she was supposed to be thinking or putting up with somebody. I told her it was Eddie. I kept my voice down. I said I was sorry. Behind me there was a sound like something had jumped onto one of the folding chairs. It scared me.

When I was little my grandmother and father took Tony out into our backyard and he crawled down a hole where they'd just had a tree stump pulled. And he started screaming because the hole turned out to be a wolf spider nest, and thousands of gray wolf spiders scrambled up him while I watched from across the yard. They covered him from the bottom up like an animated cartoon. My father and grandmother shook him out and pulled off all his clothes and hosed him down, and that night in bed he was still crying. He was kicking his arms and legs and rubbing them against the blanket and sheets. My grandmother spent the night and she and I sat up around him. He had terrible dreams, too. At one point my grandmother turned to me and said, "What can we do to help?" and we both looked at each other because we knew the answer: Almost nothing.

They'd put a rosary in her hands and the beads had shifted, spilling down the side. I thought about fixing them but I didn't. In the cellar the furnace went on. It was not completely dark. She was lying there like I would be, like Tony would be, because it was too late and didn't matter at the same time.

I touched her hand, the skin first and then the nonskin feeling underneath. I picked it up, and outside the streetlight went out, changing the quality of the darkness, and in the room things seemed to vibrate in reaction. My grandmother looked very young. In the darkness her hand came up like something rising out of a river at night. I put mine underneath hers so her fingertips fell between my knuckles. It was like when I slept with Tony on the sofa, his hand on mine, and my grandmother said when she'd seen us that one Christmas when we'd been snowed in, *Adesso tu sei la mia famiglia:* Now you are my family. But this was also not close; this was something else.

Her hand seemed patient. The clocks stopped. My hand too was floating. It was like we had nothing for those we loved but our presence, and often we didn't have that. My hand was asleep. My breathing was there for me. My connection with my grandmother was as real as our touch, and that was as certain and hard to understand as my bloodstream.

Mars Attacks

#1: *The Invasion Begins*

A bubble-helmeted Martian in the left foreground stares out at us and points at the saucer, which is silvery white and spotted along its outside rim with the black ovals of windows. The saucer stands on four narrow poles, like a tent at a wedding. A column of Martians in green spacesuits with red scuba tanks on their backs extends to a prosaic ladder leading to an open hatch. Another saucer is on the ground behind the first. An easy diagonal of saucers swoops by in the background. The sky is a deep blue, fading to an ominous yellow on the horizon. Jagged orange peaks rise in the distance on the right. The Martian's pupils are red. His whites are huge. His nose and teeth are a skull's. His brain is oversized and exposed. The back of the card is a caramel brown. On it we learn why they're doing this: buildup of atomic pressures beneath the surface of Mars with an explosion only weeks or months away, no choice, and a reckless overconfidence in the power of their weapons. We're told to *See Card #2: Martians Approaching.*

#2: Martians Approaching

Again a face looking out from the left foreground, with an excited, sheepish grin. Behind him, two other Martians, one working controls, one pointing out the window. The Martians clearly point a lot. Behind them, saucers, extending to Earth. Earth's continents are emerald green and its oceans a pale bathroom-tile color. Eastern Canada seems oversized.

#3: Attacking an Army Base

One GI, the only one not on fire, shoots up at the closest saucer. The yellow line of the bullet looks feeble, the squirt of a water pistol. All around him, his pals in agony. The saucers crowd in, jostling one another, blocking out sky. In one corner, a few bodies lying around, incinerated. On the back: *A quiet Sunday afternoon was turned to tragedy as flying saucers launched their first attack against Earth.*

#55: Mars Attacks! A Short Synopsis of the Story

Planning to conquer the Earth, Mars sends flying saucers through space carrying deadly weapons. Burning the cities, the Martians destroy much of Earth's population. The enemy then enlarges insects to over 500 times their normal size and releases them on the helpless planet. People go into hiding, knowing that death is the consequence if they are discovered by the creatures. Despite its losses, Earth launches a counterattack that shatters the Martians on their home planet, Mars. I was eight years old. Martian Cards, we called them. I filled in each box on the checklist in pencil, in case one was lost or traded. As a collector of Martian Cards, I was a figure to be reckoned with. I carried doubles to and from school wrapped in a rubber band. The nuns hated them. For a full year, they were everything. My brother and I were constantly deciding: should we pool what we had, or compete for cards? Did my parents have an opinion? What sort of gum came with them? *Did* gum come with them?

#4: *Saucers Blast Our Jets*

One saucer; nine jets. The saucer tilted in a lazy diagonal, like Maurice Chevalier's straw hat. A jet alongside it explodes in a V shape. Flying outward with the rest of the debris, a human figure. (*One of the pilots tried to get a look at the inside of a spaceship. Seeing this, the saucer smashed itself into the jet without any damage to itself.*) Delta-wing fighters chug towards the saucer from the foreground and background. Another, below, exploded by the heat ray. Its nose cone, interestingly, popping off from the impact. Another on the far right doing a fiery corkscrew to earth. Two others streaking by below, presumably part of a different, fatal, attack. *See Card #5: Washington in Flames.*

#5: *Washington in Flames*

On the back: *The Martians did not spare anyone from their vicious death rays and fear for the president's welfare continued to grow by the hour.* What happens to him? We never find out.

#6: *Burning Navy Ships*

The sky in the background is brilliant purple. Two men manning the machine gun are on fire, one showing his back, head down, as if submitting. Behind them, a white-hatted officer, raising an elbow to deflect a saucer's heat ray, squinting at its brightness. My brother calls long distance to ask if I know what these cards are worth. He was at one of the conventions; he saw a full set on one of the tables. Fifteen hundred dollars, he says. He's calling from New Orleans. He's crisscrossing the country. He stays in youth hostels, rooming houses. He's forty-two. My father wires him money—a hundred dollars, two hundred dollars—every few weeks. He rarely works, and when he does he loses the job quickly. He calls me, his only brother, the younger brother, when he's at his most despairing. His calls are monologues of defeat. I fancy myself always busy, and listen for one or two hours at a stretch, aggrieved. The only safe subject is our old collecting days: what's implicit between us is his belief that that's the only thing in his life that has panned out.

#7: *Destroying the Bridge*

Finally a good view into the top of a saucer: tiny figures in the green suits and scuba tanks facing inward, sitting in pairs around a large round table. More death rays. The sky canary yellow. The Golden Gate Bridge in scarlet. The suspension cables falling away like noodles, though the rays don't intersect with them. Tumbling cars: a red Lincoln Continental with a black roof. A green station wagon. Below, a ship flying an American flag from the bow is halved by the falling debris. *Cars plunged into the icy waters bringing death to the helpless passengers within. Screaming hysterically, the people had no way of escaping their steel coffins.* My brother, later institutionalized, was then just beginning to "act up," as my father put it. I'd recently killed my dog by running her across the street into a car. I retreated to my room for long stretches to lay the cards out and give my parents more to worry about. Did I think of the cards as a Refuge? I did not.

#10: *The Skyscraper Tumbles*

The Empire State Building breaking like a cookie, its top third tumbling off at a thirty-degree angle. The saucer responsible is out of proportion and half the building's length. The sky an electric red. Other buildings, other saucers, other fires. *New York was burning down and no one could do anything to help.* On good days I would tap the cards on my palm to line them up. Hold them under my nose to reexperience their smell: faint, musty, dry, sugary. Fan them out before me while I drank Tom Collins mix with ice and pretended it was a cocktail.

#11: *Destroy the City*

A rampart of burning bodies and skeletal remains. Vacant mouths, gaping eye sockets, tumbled rib cages. Flames issuing from a stomach cavity. In the middle ground, on a perfectly featureless street, four Martians: one erect and pointing, three charging off in the direction he indicates. They carry short, speargun-sized weapons wired to their suits. Behind them, more bodies. A factory resembling Sikorsky Aircraft, where my father worked. A smashed car. A black figure writhing in the yellow heart of a fireball. My brother would walk home from school in the middle of the day, two miles, without notifying anyone. He refused to cut his hair. He refused to sing the national anthem. During an assembly the principal brought him to the microphone and had him sing it alone. Nothing was glamorous about these rebellions; his misery with his own behavior was too transparent. He lost cards; gave them away; stopped buying. I began to pull ahead.

#13: *Watching from Mars*

A huge, circular room, not well lighted, with a polished floor. Immense curved windows and a lunar landscape beyond with moonlight (or earthlight) and another home (communication center?) in the distance. It has the overall shape of the plastic dome shielding doughnuts in a diner. In the foreground a sober Martian face considering a panel of magenta dials. Another barefoot and half-naked Martian in a curved seat offering little back support. The visible foot has three long toes. The large head and skinny limbs give the impression of early childhood. One hand holds a champagne glass full of cranberry juice. One points at a huge screen. Beside the screen, another Martian, knees bent, hands politely clasped behind his back, watching. On the screen, the Capitol Building, flanked by saucers against a blood-red sky. *Their advanced civilization had developed TV cameras which were capable of sending pictures millions of miles through space.*

#14: *Charred by Martians*

A generic tomato-red sixties convertible up on two wheels, its back end bursting into flame. The driver's arms up and head back in a Victorian tableau of distress. The saucer only a few feet overhead. Two Martians visible peeping down, like skeletal Kilroys. *The young doctor was driving home after visiting a patient when he heard a humming noise overhead. . . .*

#16: *Panic in Parliament*

Outside, a mild blue day and flying saucers. The sketchy outlines of a stately hall with the roof torn away. A large Martian grinning and firing in, suspended impossibly in the air. Panic. One man jumping down from his desk, arms spread wide. *Ironically, the topic being discussed at the time was about military plans to beat back the space invaders.* Confiscated by Sister Justine, who held it before me like an illustration of sin. Was this what I wanted for myself? she wanted to know. Was this what I aspired to? I had no idea what she meant. Later I realized they were frightened for my brother, worried that they hadn't caught whatever was happening to him in time, and anxious to avoid the same mistake with me.

#19: *Burning Flesh*

Too gross to talk about. A crouching Martian on the left, a little vacant-eyed, his death ray blooming in the belly of a man with a matinee idol's face: blue eyes, Rock Hudson hair. The man's hands cup themselves around the white light. The flesh below his shoulders and above his knees is shearing off the bone. At his feet, another skeleton with the face intact, and behind him another Martian tilting forward hesitantly, weapon raised and expression apprehensive. As if he's thinking, Whoa. Do we want to keep doing this?

#20: *Crushed to Death*

Three Martians looking down with sadistic absorption from their saucer at three men and four women being crushed between what looks like an outlandishly large snow shovel and the wall of a building. The shovel is operated by a metal arm from the saucer. The brick wall is crumbling and tumbling down, as if the bricks had never been mortared. The man closest to the wall resembles Joe E. Brown. How slow *were* these people? How'd they get caught in front of a shovel like this? *The terror caused by the flying saucers was endless. It seemed as if the Martians always had a new form of horror to inflict upon the people of Earth.* During one of my brother's recent calls I made a mark on a scratch pad for every word I contributed to the conversation. The call went fifty-five minutes and I put eleven marks on the pad. When I'm sitting down listening to him, my knee bounces like I'm keeping rhythm in a zydeco band. Among the things I volunteer occasionally when he calls: You need to see somebody professional. You need to find out how much of this is biochemical. You're not getting anywhere wandering all over the country. Among the things I never volunteer: Whenever you need or want to, call.

#21: *Prize Captive*

A horror-stricken blonde in the wraparound embrace of a Martian who's all smiles and eyes at his good fortune. She's wearing a cravat. The first bit of good news in twenty-one cards: *The girl kicked and screamed at the touch of the alien. The Martian was so startled by the woman's antics that he released her. Taking the opportunity, the girl fled.* See Card #22: *Burning Cattle*.

#22: *Burning Cattle*

#23: *The Frost Ray*

A red sun in a red sky, and six men frozen in supplicating poses. *The rays of the sun had no thawing effect at all.* In my brother's mind, I have a successful life: a home, a job, some status. Talking with me is a humiliation. The card conjures up a memory: My mother on the phone to my aunt, elaborating on my performance in the diocesan spelling bee. My cards spread in front of me on the living room rug in rows of five, with gaps for the ones still missing. My brother staring at the television set, rigid with shame.

#24: *The Shrinking Ray*

One GI charges while another, the size of his foot, shrinks. His helmet, flying off, threatens to cover him, as in a shell game. Another handheld Martian ray, this one looking like an insecticide spray. *His buddy watched horrified as the six-foot-tall man was reduced to inches, before vanishing from sight.* So was his buddy watching or charging? Do we believe our eyes or the narration? What else are we not being told?

#25: *Capturing a Martian*

The second bit of good news. A netted Martian in the foreground, his hand in a soldier's face, drawing blood. A few other soldiers stand around helpfully with their ends of the net. *A quick jab with the bayonet quieted the alien and he was carried off to Earth's military headquarters. There, trained specialists would attempt to break the language barrier and communicate with the captured Martian.*

#26: *The Tidal Wave*

A disappointment: I'd heard about the card, loved the idea. The wave was a nonmonumental swirl of blue and white, tumbling toylike ocean liners around indifferently rendered skyscrapers. Saucers in the foreground. Crumbling buildings. *The saucers' powers seemed unlimited.*

#27: *The Giant Flies*

A beetle-shaped blue thing resembling no fly we've ever seen, clutching and contemplating a helpless policeman waving a tiny gun. Two large compound eyes and curved mandibles, like tusks. Eleven other flies tumble from an overhead saucer. Humans run panicked in all directions. The sky is a lemon yellow. *The normally annoying pests were now transformed into deadly menaces, attacking any slow-footed human around.* I fought, with Gary Holter, over this card. He broke his tooth. I cut my hand. My father said, "I wouldn't be throwing those friends away. There aren't that many to go around, sport."

#29: *Death in the Shelter*

The victim Italian-looking, a cross between my uncle Guido and Richard Conte, with Latin features and curly black hair. Families cowering behind him. Beside him, inexplicably, a dead ringer for Lon Chaney in *The Phantom of the Opera*, a movie I'd already seen at that age. An *homage?* Even I wondered.

#30: *Trapped!!*
The huge spiders were perhaps the ugliest and most frightening of all the giant insects. The woman, dressed in white, entangled head to foot, has one arm above her head as if wanting to answer a question. Her head is turned away but her eyes look back at the spider. The spider, tiger-striped in red and black, holds her with three legs and has bright white pedipalps, like teeth. My father bought me the pack that contained this card and I forget which others. This I remember because of the teasing noise he made when he saw it, knowing I was afraid of spiders.

#31: *The Monster Reaches In*
Lost. What I remember: Another blonde wrapped in an embrace, the double green tarsus of an insect reaching through a window. A leg reaches farther in for a soldier, whose bayonet opens a lawn sprinkler of blood along its length.

#32: *Robot Terror*
A greenish robot like a squat peppermill with arms. Three arms: one with a vacuumlike attachment that's already sucked up half a human; two with pincerlike claws, one of which is driven deep into the center of a swooning young woman in a sundress. It rolls along on low, spiked wheels. On its side, rivets. In its head, a Martian, who looks genuinely sympathetic.

#33: *Removing the Victims*
By some means the aliens had found a way to communicate with the giant insects they had created. The bugs followed any in-

struction given to them by the spacemen. Did the bugs want anything in return? Could humans hear their talk? Were the negotiations difficult? More mysteries.

#8: *Terror in Times Square.* #9: *The Human Torch.* #12: *Death in the Cockpit.* #15: *Saucers Invade China.* #17: *Beast and the Beauty.* #18: *A Soldier Fights Back.* #35: *The Flame Throwers.* #38: *Victims of the Bug.* #40: *High Voltage Execution.* #41: *Horror in Paris.* #42: *Hairy Fiend.* One afternoon Sister Justine confiscated eleven cards from Milton Dietz. For three days she had them in her desk. On the fourth day while I watched from the boys' bathroom she pitched them into the dumpster. That night I got them back with a flashlight, one leg sunk into someone's applesauce from lunch. Milton was crushed at the loss, but I didn't return them. Worse: I didn't confess it to Father Hogan. Who knew how closely he worked with the nuns?

#34: *Terror in the Railroad*

A gigantic ant, fire-engine red, filling a curved rail shed, embracing with three of its six legs a lighted green railway car, and crushing the top of it in its jaws. My parents worry that when they're dead I'll inherit their job as my brother's keeper. My brother has no one else. That leaves them unhappy when he's in contact with me and unhappy when he's not. I maintain the disingenuous position of the good son, offering to do more and deferring to the wisdom of their greater caution. Bodies tumble out of the connecting railway cars. One is outlined with ragged and filigreed white light, suggesting the third rail. *The entire station was thrown into a panic as they watched the fascinated insect crush several cars the way a child might crush a toy he had grown tired of.*

#36: *Destroying a Dog*

The boy shrieks as he runs to prevent it, both fists raised in protest like a figure on a left-wing poster. The dog a cross between a German shepherd and a golden retriever. The dog's coat flies to pieces under the force of the ray, separating like autumn leaves off a pile in the wind. The little mail flag on the mailbox is down.

#37: *Creeping Menace*

Two men sprinting past demolished rural buildings. One man carrying a small boy in a red shirt and white socks. The boy seems to want to tell him something. The giant insect right behind them is indigo with cherry-red eyes.

#39: *Army of Giant Insects*

An entomological Guadalcanal: in the foreground, GIs armed with cannons, bazookas, machine guns, and rifles, the NCO exhorting them to hold the line; in the background, an oncoming storm of insects as far as the eye can see. Air Force jets overhead offer support. One bug flies up into the air backwards out of the mass. One of the hardest cards to find, and it had to be replaced, at the cost of three months: my brother held it up in front of me early one morning, when I was still in bed, and tore it into eighths.

#43: *Blasting the Bug*

The bug's leg resting with a casual friendliness on the front of a tank that blasts its compound eye at point-blank range. Two soldiers hurl grenades. One holds out his palm as if to reason with everyone. Everything floats on an undifferentiated red background. We all went out for lunch the day of my brother's institutionalization, before he was to be dropped off. He answered questions monosyllabically. It was the worst day of my parents' lives. At some point my father went to pay the check. My mother went to help. I didn't blame her. My brother and I sat around the ruins of our chili dogs. "I put all my cards and stuff in boxes upstairs," he told me. "Don't let them screw around with them."

I nodded. That night my mother cried her way around the house and ended up in his room. She was rearranging things, packing things. Was she messing up what he'd organized? I couldn't go up to find out. At dawn I crept into his room and found his shoeboxes arranged on the floor of his closet. Was that the way he'd left them? Were they all there? I looked at his Martian cards: eleven I already owned. One I didn't—#28: *Helpless Victim.* A perverse love scene: a giant insect and young boy lying alongside one another, a mandible poised at the jugular, the boy trying to avert his head, his mouth open in protest. I took the card and closed the box. I'd return it when—or if, I thought, crouching on the floor of his closet—my brother came back.

#44: *Battle in the Air*

A red Sikorsky helicopter, an old S-58, and a fat, ludicrous flying bug the same color. Below, monochromatic suburban homes. An attempt at stylization? Saving on colors? A shot from a rifleman on board deflects something issuing from the bug: A tongue of some sort? A stream of fire?

#45: *Fighting Giant Insects*

Better production values. The soldiers' helmets look German. A bazooka in one place draws thick black blood. A bayonet in another draws white. The insect has a body of black fur. How much research was done for this series? Were there things like this in the Amazon?

#46: *Blastoff for Mars*

Without explanation, Earth takes the offensive. In a forest of Cape Canaverals, whole formations of men and tanks clamber up ramps directly into the exhaust cones of liquid-fueled rockets. Other rockets streak by on a diagonal. White smoke billows out in various directions. What are the Martians doing while all this is happening? Where are the giant insects? *Men from the ages of 16 to 45 were given quick physical examinations and enlisted into the Earth Army.*

#47: *Earth Bombs Mars*

The bombardier's fingers bring back a photo of a family vacation in Montauk. Who took the picture? My mother slung in a low sand chair, squinting grimly out to sea. My father demonstrating how to add a tower to a rambling sand castle. Behind him, my brother and I squatting over something on our scratchy old Army blanket: cards, two new packages each, that my father bought us at the drugstore near the beach.

#48: *Earthmen Land on Mars*

Another purple sky. Parachutists coming down, a huge Earth behind them. The horizon curves sharply. The ground is arid and broken by palisades. Martians are running toward us. One who's being shot in the head from behind is tilting delicately toward the shot. He's wearing a close-fitting shirt with pointed padded shoulders and bikini briefs. Another, about to run out of the frame, is all brain and bulging eyes. Don't the Martians have radar? Is this all a trap?

#49: *The Earthmen Charge*

Soldiers with red standard-issue helmets under glass mill around a tank porcelain-white like a Frigidaire. Otherwise they wear regular khakis. Why aren't they cold? Or hot? How does the glass form a seal? On their backs, the same red scuba tanks the Martians wore, but no regulators, and no air hoses. In the distance, a domed city out of the Jetsons, with air taxis and floating platforms. A monorail toots out toward them. Are the Martian commuters puzzled as to what's going on? *The leader of the troop gave his orders and the soldiers continued toward the dome, with revenge in their hearts.*

#50: *Smashing the Enemy*

A soldier whose helmet reads US on the front drives the butt of his rifle into a charging Martian's brain. A buddy at his side sporting a Norwegian flag drives his bayonet into another Martian's eye. All of this takes place on an immense flight of stairs. One Martian attacks with what appears to be a vegetable peeler. Where are the heat rays? Where are the forces in reserve? Where is the Martian National Guard?

#51: *Crushing the Martians*

A Martian in the foreground losing all his dentition. Another dead in the middle ground and leaking a winding stream of blood. A small boy's notion of the ultimate tank, bristling with cannons pointed in all directions, breaks through the aquarium wall of the dome and fires. At my brother's confirmation I sat in the car after the ceremony and traded for this card, with a cousin I rarely saw. My brother was wildly unhappy. The scrutiny was excruciating to him. Waiting in line for the bishop's blessing, he pawed at his suit, his haircut, his eyes. He spent the ceremony crying and enraged at himself for doing so. My parents were frozen with mortification.

Afterwards they dispensed with the photos in front of the church. They couldn't get my brother to come back to the car.

My mother found me in the backseat and told me she didn't
know what they were going to do. My cousin was embarrassed for
us. My mother wanted me to help however I could, and I knew
it. I could see my brother yank his arm away from my father
across the parking lot. I had no idea what I could or couldn't accomplish. I was too frightened to find out. Meanwhile, here was
my cousin: he lived nowhere near me, so I knew he'd have different cards.

#52: *Giant Robot*
   Silly. Buttons for eyes, transformers for antennae, wrench-grip
pliers for hands. No one's even wearing helmets or oxygen tanks
anymore. *An Army bazooka hit its mark, and the robot crumbled
disabled to the ground.*

#53: *Martian City in Ruins*
   *Martian victims were sprawled across the desert sands, many
badly wounded and others beyond repair. The advanced civilization had been beaten into the dust under the force of Earth's vio-
lent counterattack. The dangerous atomic pressures were rapidly
building to the climactic point and it was now only hours before
the explosion which would destroy Mars. See Card #54: Mars Explodes.*

#54: *Mars Explodes*
   The end of the series. Collecting took a year. What was the
first card? *Death in the Shelter.* I pored over it at night under the
covers, cupped it in my hands at Mass, laid it on my thigh, school
days, in the boys' bathroom. What did it connect to? What was
the rest of the story? I had no synopsis and had seen no other
cards. Everything lay ahead of me. I was hooked when I saw the
first one. A giant bug, eating a guy: that was for me. My parents

did what they could. They were attentive; they were flexible. Who knows if they trace their disappointment with me back that far?

What was the last card? *Watching from Mars.* Months of searching, and it was my brother who finally found it. A few weeks after the doctors let him come home, he left it on my desk, with a note: *For your collection.* In the meantime, I'd lost *The Monster Reaches In.* When he calls now, and tells me what the set's going for, I tell him I don't have the set; I lost one. And he says, Yeah, you have the set. Remember? I found the last one. *Watching from Mars.*

And it kills me that he remembers the title. It kills me that I can't bring myself to keep talking to him, to tell him, No, I don't have the whole set.

Now I'm trying to remember: Did I ever have them all or not? Did they further separate me from my family, or allow me a place within it? Did I know then how much they affected what I could imagine? Do I know now? But that was how I learned how to see, and that was what I saw.

Ida

Millions roar. The Three Rivers Stadium scoreboard lights up, the thick letters turning the rectangle from black to yellow: DEE-FENSE. DEE-FENSE. Over the line the Pittsburgh Steelers hunch taut, ready to explode. I straighten up. Time out! I call, Time out! and trot to the sidelines. My father waits, his arms folded. He didn't want the time-out used; against Pittsburgh we'll need them later.

Greenwood and Dwight White are way wide, I explain. He doesn't say anything. The corners are in tight, I add a little desperately, I think it's a dog. My mother trots over, stands beside me for support, lets her mouthpiece slip from her mouth. He waits agonizing seconds more before answering.

Okay, he says. Go with Ida here on the blast.

It's the wrong call, the worst call, but I don't argue; I turn and jog back onto the field. The crowd seems to swell physically in the stands. The Steelers sidle back to their positions. I'm standing in the dark brilliant purple of a Minnesota Viking huddle in a 1975 championship game, and the Steelers, the home team, are already in black. None of this is strange to me. The colors, the rich purple against the black, seem right, the way it should be. We've earned this spot. I have no memory of who we beat to get here, but we've earned this spot.

In the huddle my mother bends at the waist, slips her mouthpiece back in, doesn't look up as I call her number. On the way out of the huddle she straightens her face mask angrily, uselessly.

At the snap Greenwood roars in, Ham fills the gap beside him and, hurtling the line, meets my mother head-on in the opening we both knew would be, cruelly, not an opening at all but an avenue for the oncoming blitz. She is savaged backward, driven into and across the cold artificial surface, and again I think, That's it, she's finished. I wave to the sidelines, motioning toward my mother, but my father remains oblivious; no replacement starts out onto the field.

I curse. I gesture theatrically. Why is he doing this to her? I call another time-out, for her sake. On the way to the sidelines I see him throw his hands up in the air and turn his back to me.

Once there I unsnap my chin strap and lick my first three fingers, peering at the scoreboard while I talk with my uncle. We're in the fourth quarter and there's no score. We haven't been able to move because my mother has gotten every call and the Steelers are ready for her and us each time. My uncle tells me she has fifty-six carries for seventeen yards. We have seventeen yards total offense. The Steelers have not scored because their offense is not allowed on the field. When we have to punt, we receive the ball we've punted. The Steelers know they've been cheated. They're frustrated and meaner than usual and they've started gambling on every play. They're blitzing a lot and hitting late and grabbing at the ball, but my mother's fumbled only once in fifty-six carries, and I fell on it. Thank you, Son, she'd said, with great dignity, rising from her knees after we'd all unpiled.

The Pittsburgh crowd, too, senses the injustice; they're loud and bitter and they roar with delight when my mother receives each assault. The sound itself seemed to slow our reflexes the one time they saw the ball squirt straight up, a comic, precious seed, the one time my mother fumbled.

Hey, my uncle is saying. Let's go. I head back across the field to my teammates. It's second and eleven. They watch me, their eyes pleading this one time for a pass. My uncle's signals from the sidelines, though, are clear: Ida on the 23 Pitch. I anger when they sag, and snap at them irritably: Maybe if we worked a little harder we could spring her.

My mother bends, exhausted, to her three-point stance.

Over the line I can see Lambert inching to the right. Mean Joe Greene, too, inches over. They're all waiting, peering up at me from lowered helmets. I won't let it happen again, I think, but at the snap the ball is out of my hands, flipping end over end, before I've realized it, my pitch hitting my mother perfectly in the midsection seconds before Lambert and Greene and Mel Blount bury her.

Sprawled across the artificial surface, our team despairs. My mother lies on her back, eyes closed to the gray Pittsburgh sky, wheezing painfully. Kneeling over her, I call another time-out, and my father explodes on the far sidelines, flinging his clipboard past the ducking heads of caped Vikings.

On the sidelines with him I try it again. They're wide open for play action and Foreman or Gilliam deep. We're both looking out at the teams, my mother kneeling, her head down, her hands on her thighs.

Go with the pitch again, he says. First we establish the run.

This time, no. I almost say it aloud to Lambert, across the line.

His missing front teeth make his eyeteeth fangs. I glance back at my mother already in her stance. She'd accepted the call without reaction. This will be fifty-eight carries.

She takes the pitch and veers unexpectedly away from our blocking and has almost five yards on the sheer boldness of her cut before lowering her head and taking on Mel Blount helmet to helmet. In the impact, she spins off helpless, absurdly frail, into a slash of Pittsburgh tacklers, the ball punched free and jerking past me, rolling innocent toward our goal line, and a host of Steelers are after it, Greenwood, Greene, Ham, and, running alongside, I can't even reach the one—Greenwood—who finally gets control of it and carries it aloft into the end zone, the sound from the Pittsburgh fans coming down at us like thunder.

I crouch over my mother, on the bench. Blood is flecked in tiny red dots across the white of her face mask. I'm sorry, she says. I had it, but it must've popped out when they hit me.

This is finished, I think. He's got to listen.

But he's stone on the sidelines, watching the kickoff team swarmed over, listening to the headset. No, he answers suddenly. We're only six down. Run her on some misdirection. He stares into me. She's a professional, he says. She gets paid to do this.

Pittsburgh's waiting for the misdirection, too, and Greene drives her onto her back so that the people on the sidelines can hear the impact.

Mom, I say over her, and I start to cry. She swims in my vision, her head lolling from side to side. I wave, stand and wave, enraged in mime, but no replacement comes. My mother gets back on her feet. I lean into the huddle. I want to call a pass, but I can't: Gilliam, Lash, Voigt, they're all avoiding my eyes, and I have no faith in my arm. We haven't worked on any of this.

So I call the 23 Pitch to my mother and move down the line at the snap only to plant and cut rather than pitching, Lambert's astonished face flashing by, my teammates shouting, whooping, pounding along behind in useless support before Mel Blount slants in on me inexorably and slams me down as a betrayer, a cheat, riding up and over me in his anger as we tumble along the sidelines.

The crowd, stunned, erupts anyway, after a pause. It is the first first down of the game. My father is frantically trying to signal a time-out but he can't, we've used them all, I've used them all.

That's like you, Dad, I think, bringing the team back to the huddle. But we're not listening now. My teammates look at me with new hope, a new sense of possibility, and I call my own number again. At the snap I'm swarmed under, astounded at the viciousness of the tackles, hobbled. I hold my knee. Lambert stands over me, nodding. No more diagonal cuts.

I limp to my feet, my father sends a replacement out for me, I wave him back. All the anger and frustration hits and I'm near tears again, the crossbars in the distant Steeler end zone mocking us over their helmets. We'll never get this in, I think bitterly. My mother, leaning forward in the huddle, hands on thighs, says, It's okay.

I look into her eyes in fear and wonder, and I want to show her I love her, want to demonstrate how much support she has from me, if not physical, now, then mental, emotional; want desperately for my support to help.

Call the play, she says. Everyone's waiting.

23 Pitch, I say.

She takes it and is driven out-of-bounds, into spectators, yard markers, the bench. Equipment flies. She returns to the huddle breathing noisily from her mouth. Call it again, she says. She lowers her head, drives forward, collides with Blount, staggers, and keeps going. The referee signals first down, and I rush over and hug her to her feet. She still has not let go of the ball. In the huddle she sways slightly. Run it again, she whispers.

And she drives forward again and again, exchanging yards for the punishment her body absorbs until the Steeler goalposts loom high above us.

There're two minutes left, she says. Her teeth, in the huddle, are red. Time-out is given to both benches for the two-minute warning, and my father is halfway out onto the field, trying to get us over to the sideline.

I look at her closely. We don't have to go, I remind her. He's still the coach, she says. And I want to get these taped up. She stares critically at her hand, the smaller two fingers dangling uselessly, flapping a bit as she walks.

They wrap my mother's hand while my uncle yells tendencies, patterns, picked up from up in the booth, in my ear. My father, who'd been desperate to get us to the sidelines, seems unable to speak. He grabs my arm, then my mother's, and gesticulates. He seems overwhelmed. I feel content, surprised and pleased and superior. My mother raises her hand to signal enough, and they snip the tape. Now listen to what Coach said, my uncle reminds us. We trot back out onto the pale green expanse, our teammates, the Steelers, millions waiting.

The scoreboard flashes STOP, then IDA. STOP—IDA. The crowd responds, picking up the chant.

I hug her again, my teammates embarrassed, bewildered, our helmets clacking together earhole to earhole, and tell her, They can't. I know that now. When I let her go she looks at me as though I still have more to learn.

The lights are on above the stadium rim, reflecting in yellow circles off the high-gloss purple of her helmet, refracting in the scars in the plastic. The sky is blue-black and a wind picks up. Across the line, hands on hips, Greenwood shivers.

I call the play. Halfway down to her stance, my mother says behind me, Either we do it here or we don't do it at all.

The scoreboard announces, belatedly, that my mother's sixty-six carries are a National Football League record. The crowd boos.

I pitch it and my mother gains three yards, leaping and being cartwheeled in midair, bouncing on her shoulder.

I pitch it and she gains three more, cutting back inside, her head snapping around as her face mask is grabbed and her body flies out from under her.

And she carries again, and again. Once more, she says in the huddle, coughing, and over center I realize the Steelers are crouching in their own end zone, and there are eight men up on the line of scrimmage, thighs quivering, ready to shoot every gap. The stadium clock shows five seconds remaining and I find myself wondering where the time went.

I pitch it a final time, both hands supplicating as they follow the flight of the ball, and the Steelers have her completely shut off to the sideline, and as she plants her foot to cut, Lambert's helmet catches her flush in the face and Greenwood's in the chest, and she's knocked five yards backward in a splinter of face-mask pieces, catching herself with her free hand, somehow keeping her balance, reversing herself, heading instinctively, blindly, for the opposite sideline, gaining speed as she runs back past me, face bloody, eyes closed, jagged pieces of face mask jutting out from the helmet. I spin and head for the end zone, her only blocker, most of our teammates down and the Steelers having overpursued to the other side of the field. There's only Blount and as he throws himself at my mother I throw myself at him, and we pile up, brutally, my mother underneath with the ball over the goal line.

My teammates mob her, and I'm caught in the crush, still tangled with Blount, and the coaching staff mobs her, baldheaded, paunchy men leaping and shrieking among the purple of the uniforms, and the Steelers are shoving people around, and suddenly I'm scared for her. She's up on somebody's shoulders and I try to fight my way over to her but I can't, and I start shouting her name and she turns and sees me. Across the field my father stands alone in the horizontal expanse of the empty sideline, surveying his clipboard, and above him the scoreboard announces fifteen more minutes, and the start of a fifth quarter. Mom! I yell over the noise. Mom! We've still got overtime! She yells something back and I can't hear it and try to fight closer, and she says, It never really will stop. We got to get a handle on it anyway, and as the mob carries her back toward our sideline my throwing arm and knee recover and surge with energy, as if looking forward to their supporting role.

Piano Starts Here

We were trying to see a dog that could've been dead already and we weren't getting anywhere, Susan said. We were standing outside her veterinarian's office in a four a.m. drizzle. My hair felt like wet old clothes on my neck. Susan's breath ghosted the glass. She had asked to be let in, and the boy inside had not yet responded. He gazed at us vacantly, his mop handle teetering, running water shifting and realigning his image on the pane. Susan spread a hand across it, as if to push through. She had twice explained that her dog was in there and that the doctor had given her permission to come down so late. The boy seemed to have trouble focusing.

Doppleresque trucks rushed and whined on the interstate in the distance. The boy palmed the door handle with an appealing gentleness. He puffed his cheeks like a bugler, and turned the latch. The door swung outward.

"Audrey," Susan said, once inside. "A beagle mix. She hasn't come out of the anesthetic."

The boy did not respond. He led us through a second door. Susan's boots made amphibious sounds on the tile.

Audrey was still on the table. She had been brought in earlier unable to stand on her hind legs. Cortisone had been no help. The decision had been made to operate and they had found a lesion impinging on the spinal cord. The recommendation was to let her go. That was the veterinarian's phrase. Susan was taking the night to think it over.

Audrey had not revived from the anesthetic and was not a good bet to do so. She lay on her side with her midsection shaved and bandaged. One paw hung from the table.

"I came in and checked earlier," the boy said. "She hasn't moved."

Susan gave him a wan smile. "Audie-feeber," she said. "Old Audrey-feen." She sounded like the loser on a quiz show. She squatted near the dog and put her fingers against its nose. "Here we got our big numbers tomorrow and where will you be?"

Our recital in Adult Music was the next afternoon at three.

We had signed up together eleven weeks previous. Susan had kept her distance from me, and that was something I hoped to change. Friends scoffed and remained casual about the possibilities, musical or romantic. They admitted that they themselves rarely did that which was in their best interests, whether because of the kids or work or general laziness. Around me they seemed both distracted and skeptical, as if always aware of neglected parallel tracks of richer possibility.

Susan and I showed zero aptitude for the instrument. I had no ability. Susan flustered and grew frustrated and banged the keys like someone losing an argument. For us the keyboards stretched limitless in each direction, and the keys lay in quiet and narrow rows as individual as grains of rice. We had both, it turned out (Susan saw nothing interesting in the coincidence), abandoned the instrument in childhood, spurning the loneliness of solitary application to music, I theorized, for yet another sort. We had sat imprisoned with stereotypic piano teachers in dark parlors, reinventing simple exercises, sweating and hesitant, imagining a world of joy and laughter beyond our windows while our hands produced a series of remorseless sounds.

The patterns returned to our adult lives in the singsong cadences of nonachievement: *Every Good Boy Deserves Favor. All Cows Eat Grass. Big Dogs Fight All Cats.* We behaved as true believers trusting that refusing to confront the catastrophe might yet reverse it.

Susan and Audrey arrived at the North Adams Congregational Church hall that first day in my company, though she specified for the benefit of our instructor that we were not attached. She taught fourth- and fifth-level high-school history, she said, and for what? Her last group's PSATs were so low, she said, she'd recommended to one kid, when he had asked where he should go to school, the University of Mars. She was getting burnt out, in other words.

"Well, let's see what happens," she said, and cracked her knuckles theatrically. Audrey laid a chin on the piano bench.

We stood ready at that point to commit ourselves to eleven weeks of Adult Music and become part of a group seemingly already dispirited by a lack of adults. Mrs. Proekopp, our instructor, assured us she'd add younger people if necessary to fill out the class. She gestured as evidence towards a tiny child waiting wide-eyed with her mother by the front door.

The church hall had been rented for the occasion, and Mrs. Proekopp had not put herself out. Upright pianos were arranged back to back on the maroon linoleum, and the effect was that of a dismal and half-realized Busby Berkeley number.

Mrs. Proekopp had speculated right off the bat that the dog would naturally be a disruption and in the future would be better off and no doubt happier at home, and Susan had suggested that she would be the judge of that, thank you, and when the dog disturbed anyone they would let her know. Audrey had yawned.

The few other students had looked on with interest. Susan believed in serious rudeness when people in her opinion refused to see or speak clearly.

"We need something, I guess," she allowed that first day.

"You never know what you can do until you try," I told her, settling into the piano beside hers. Audrey shot me a look.

"Then you do," Susan said. "That's the problem." She lifted the index card with her name penciled on it from the fallboard. "Makes me feel like a kid again," she said, and played four notes, *plink plank plonk plunk*, and squinted at the music sheet.

I watched her hands rehearsing and re-rehearsing their intended patterns above the keyboard, her brow furrowed in puzzlement. She stared at the music like someone facing crisis in an exotic land trying to read the instructions on the emergency gear.

Her problem, she said, was that she didn't like what she'd done with herself and she didn't like what she was doing. "*One* problem, anyway," she added. The situation demanded change.

There on the first day of Getting Acquainted with Our Instruments even basic techniques remained blandly elusive. The exercises drifted serenely around my attempts to order them. Susan at one point compared the effect to that of a system created by random generation. We did not improve. Audrey lay under the piano bench, dreamily twitching.

The second day the tiny girl in the doorway, Mary Alice, was admitted to the group, and Susan told her, by way of explaining me, "He thinks he's in love with me." Mary Alice looked uncertain as to how to handle the information. After a moment or two she regarded me unsympathetically. I suggested by my expression that I didn't need the sympathy of children.

At the break we sniffed coffee in Styrofoam cups and lingered near the doughnuts. Mrs. Proekopp kept a wary eye on Audrey, who nosed the air around the tray experimentally.

"There's a difference between believing in things and refusing to see," Susan said. "You've got that love-at-first-sight thing going in your head right now; I can see it. Forget it. You and me, we're not made for each other. We're just not."

I suggested that it wasn't something that needed deciding right then.

"It's *been* decided," Susan said. "Smell the coffee, pal."

"It isn't a wholly rational process," I said. She made a squeaking noise with her lips.

"You're something," she said. "Your mouth's writing checks your behind can't cash." We drifted back to our pianos. I did a little fingering and the doughnut grease left filmy fingerprints on the ebony keys.

Between sessions we met coincidentally in a garage. Her tired orange Opel hatchback balked in the cold, she reported. Desmond, her mechanic, told her to just leave the checkbook.

I was sitting in a red plastic chair in the waiting room, waiting for my own bad news. In the garage area proper, dog dishes spotted the cement floor.

"For the rats," Susan explained. "This place is Rat Motel." I pulled up my feet.

In the Pan Tree across the street we sat in the window so we could watch our cars slowly come apart. Susan slurped her Constant Comment and watched Desmond poke disinterestedly under the Opel's hood. Audrey remained upright and stoic in the backseat, resembling at that distance the mysterious figures in the windows of suspense movies.

"You don't know me," she said. "We never dated. I have B.O. I'm always pissed off at something. I'm not your dream girl." She looked away, and I was encouraged. "All this interest is sad, you know?"

I asked about a piece of hers in the *Advocate* entitled "Jazz Giants Snub the Berkshires." Her thesis had been that they had no place to play, so it was inevitable. We talked about the older greats: Jelly Roll Morton, Art Tatum, Fatha Hines, Willie the Lion Smith. I was frequently pretending to appreciations I didn't have. She tried to make comprehensible Tatum's sixteenth-note runs at up-tempo. We considered ways of improving articulation. We had very little idea what we were talking about.

The garage lights went on across the street. "There you go, Desmond," she called to the window. "He's given up going by feel," she said to me. People in the restaurant were looking.

"Want to go to the Blind Pig?" I asked. "For a drink?"

"I don't know." Susan sighed. She made binoculars with her hands and looked at me through them. "What am I doing? What are you doing?"

"You're teaching, and writing for the *Advocate*," I said. "That could be exciting."

She nodded, her eyes on the garage. "They got me covering a guy who does gun-rack art," she said.

I folded the paper around my pumpkin muffins. I asked if she remembered the little girl, Amanda, from the last Fourth of July. Once it had gotten dark Amanda had wandered over and stood next to us petting Audrey while the fireworks boomed and popped over our heads. Her mouth had been open and the lights warmed our faces. Susan spoke quietly with her. Someone took us for a family. Amanda leaned back, her palm leaving Audrey and patting air. Look at the noise! she said. Look at the noise! Susan had lifted her up, as if for a closer look. I thought then that we were both happy. I thought, She's usually unhappy, and I'm usually unhappy. I called her after that, tried to shop where she shopped.

"I remember her," Susan said. "Beautiful girl."

The cars still weren't ready an hour later, so we walked the strip to the Artery Arcade. From the benches in front of the Zayres we could see over the Department of Motor Vehicles to Mount Greylock. Susan rubbed her eyes industrially with her fingertips. She said, "I'm thirty-three already. Billy DeBerg was sixteen years ago."

"Billy DeBerg?" I asked. She did not elaborate.

There was an immense and distant crash, as though someone had dropped a carton of bedpans.

"Fat," she said sadly, as if that followed.

"You're very beautiful," I said. This kind of talk did not come easily to me and I tried to list specifics.

"Right here," she said. With two fingers and a thumb she pinched her hip and twisted it. "Miss Cushions."

I had no comeback for that. Audrey deflected some of the awkwardness by scratching herself. Susan told some Audrey stories. The dog ate the spines of books, and at the age of eleven still urinated with joy when Susan came back from school.

"*Don't* you?" she asked. Audrey's tail thumped. We sat with her unperturbed silence as our model. The world seemed to be rewarding restraint only incrementally, but I refused on my part to push things. I had the patience of a coral reef.

Mrs. Proekopp informed us two weeks later that she wasn't pleased with our progress and could not believe, after hearing my hands skitter like frightened crabs across the keyboard, that I had been diligent in my practicing.

"Come now," she said, looking over her glasses at me. "Do you think you would sound like that if you practiced?"

I looked helplessly at my hands.

"Listen," she said. "Mary Alice, play the piece." Mary Alice straightened up and her tiny frame hunched forward. She peered at the music and began. Her version was not very good, but it was a resounding improvement. She appeared to be five to seven years old.

Mrs. Proekopp was not one to tread lightly on a point. "Did yours sound like that?" she asked, unnecessarily. "Class? Did his sound like that?" Around me neutral murmurs, blank looks. "Susan," she said. "Has he been practicing?"

"It doesn't sound like it," Susan said.

"Class," Mrs. Proekopp concluded, with an excess of élan, "we are not going to get anywhere"—she thumped my shoulder for emphasis—"not anywhere, if we do not p-r-a-c-t-i-c-e."

On the chalkboard as we entered the hall every afternoon were separate lists for each student which our instructor had entitled WHAT WE NEED TO WORK ON. Susan and I by week three were not on the board. We attributed this to a lack of space.

"Have you thought there might be other girls out there looking for you?" she said during one session, looking at her hands.

"I like *you*," I said. She bared her teeth at the music book.

"I don't know what to do with you two," Mrs. Proekopp said. Mrs. Bunteen, an elderly widow from Adams, looked on, the lights glazing her glasses. "Neither of you seem able to accomplish the smallest things with a keyboard."

"You're being too hard," I said, in Susan's defense.

"Prove it," she said. She believed herself to be, she confided, a whiz at motivation.

The room was silent. I realized I had the opportunity at that point to play for the two of us, to redeem weeks of performance with one flourish and show up the instructor. I began without taking a breath and my fingers spilled around with a palsied urgency. Mrs. Proekopp granted me a short grace period and then walked around the piano to bring an ear closer to the atrocities. Slowly and clearly she called out the missed notes like a public autopsy: B flat. G flat. B flat. B flat. At a tricky bridge I stopped, some fingers still trembling. I imagined for my hands the most grotesque punishments.

Mrs. Proekopp had by that time been reduced to grim little noises. Susan and I had been doing daily violence to the Minuet in G for two weeks. Mrs. Bunteen had begun to master the piece in six days. Mary Alice in three. Mrs. Proekopp crossed to the doughnut table and from her satchel pulled a sheaf of dittoed pages, which she divided between Susan and myself.

"Here," she said. "Take these home."

Susan leafed through the first few, pale. Centered on the page before her was a small cartoon figure of a smiling quarter note. *Hi there,* he was saying. *I'm B flat.*

She agreed to dinner, at her place, after practice—circling the wagons, she called it. We sat on the living room sofa, Audrey snoring on one end, and looked out on the erratically shingled roof next door. We had a lot of California wine. *Mr. Smith Goes to Washington* was on cable. On the jacket of an album I pulled from behind her stereo Art Tatum was making a thumbs-up sign and grinning, under the title *Piano Starts Here.*

She apologized for the cork in the wine and said we should have more because of it. She laughed at the movie and made fun

of a woman in a commercial who worried about feminine pro-
tection. During a Miller Lite ad she asked unexpectedly about
football pads. "I never figured out where the pads went, exactly,"
she said. The knees, I said. The thighs, the hips, the tailbone.
She made a face and said I wasn't being too specific.

So I traced the outline of a knee pad around her knee. I traced
the broader shape of the thigh pad. I showed her where on the
hips.

She was looking at me, serious. My hands described around
her head the narrowed globe of the helmet, my fingers outlining
the full cage of the face mask.

Audrey sighed and turned onto her back. The commercial
ended. Susan put her glass down and her legs flexed and resettled
like beautiful animals. She relaxed, a little sadder, I thought. A
frazzled Jimmy Stewart filibustered on the floor of the Senate.
His head was lowered in close-up, and he examined letters in his
hand. He mentioned lost causes. Claude Rains, sitting nearby,
looked uncomfortable.

I woke in the darkness disoriented. I was on the sofa. Susan
poked a coverlet under my chin like a bib, her frizzed hair sil-
houetted against the lamplight from her bedroom. I could hear
Audrey lapping water faintly in the distance.

"My Boy Senator," she said. "We sure bring a lot to the party,
don't we?"

Around week eight of our lessons Audrey began to have difficulty
rising after any time at all off her feet, and Susan worried about
her getting old and stiffening up. Mrs. Proekopp posted her
recital decisions. I was paired with Mary Alice—five-year-old
Mary Alice—in a duet. If it was an effort to hide me it could only
have been spectacularly unsuccessful.

Mary Alice was no happier with the arrangement and in fact

claimed equal humiliation. We resolved to make the best of it and huddled in one corner of the hall to schedule extra practice sessions, miserable Mary Alice in her MOZART sweatshirt trying distractedly to remember which days her mother could provide a ride, which days her father could pick her up. On the third emergency meeting she pounded the keys with startling force, crying "No No No No No No," and asked herself, as though I wasn't there, "What am I gonna *do?*"

Things got worse. Susan's improvement was imperceptible, and my fingers moved like sinkers as we hurtled towards our recital. She called and said something was wrong, Audrey wasn't getting up, she couldn't reach the vet, and when I went over, there was Audrey pained and sheepish over an inability to rise, pulling herself slightly this way and that in the hopes of lessening Susan's distress. The operation was authorized. Audrey was passed from arm to arm in the veterinarian's office and seemed bemused when I last saw her, before the doors shut us out.

We stood at the Greylock Animal Hospital before Audrey, packaged like an animal coming apart, and the boy with the mop said he had a lot of cleaning to do, and turned away. The four a.m. stillness amplified sounds. He went through the cabinets and poured Janitor in a Drum quietly into a clean yellow bucket, hushing the sound by easing the liquid down the tilted edge as though drawing a beer. The smell filled the air around us. On the far side of the room the animals in their holding cages were quiet. Their nails made occasional and light sounds on the metal screens of the doors.

The boy's mop slid across the floor in even strokes, renewing the shine. The tile gleamed in streaks. We all listened to Audrey breathing. The boy worked around in the sterilizer, organizing the instruments. They glittered and clashed musically in the drawers. He wiped the counter and then his hands and left the room.

Audrey's bandage looked unwieldy and impractical. Her exhalations were a quiet rasp. Her muzzle trembled. Susan ran her hand over the ribs. A drop from the nose ran onto the stainless steel. Her whiskers moved briefly, and she smelled of the anesthesia and the medicated bandage.

Susan lifted her hand. The dog seemed dead, but I wondered if there was some check we could do. She asked, finally, for the collar, and the license jingled weakly when I took it off. The boy went back in when we left, and behind us there was the flat sliding sound of Audrey being pulled from the table. I wondered if he should move her before the vet looked at her, just to be sure. I kept the thought to myself. In the car Susan's only words had to do with whether I needed a lift to the recital, and I rode beside her all the way back with an overwhelming sense of what I could and couldn't do.

By the time of the recital it was raining. Susan's Opel, a sad mustard color in that weather, broke down, and she had to walk the last four blocks. She sat beside me in the wings of the makeshift stage with her hair dripping. The collar of her new black blouse was floppy and soaked. The recital crowd was small and uncertainly enthusiastic, as if the rain might have changed everything.

Susan was represented in the audience by Desmond, who looked apologetic, and an old boyfriend. The boyfriend's name was Kevin, and he looked more uncomfortable than I was. He looked at me with the unalloyed hatred of someone with no chance considering someone else in very much the same position.

Introduced, I walked to my piano, bowing unsteadily beside

Mary Alice, her brown hair jumbled into an oversized pink bow. We sat down to our minuet. Unhappy Kevin two rows back seemed to wish the piano would detonate. Mary Alice's parents projected sympathy.

Mary Alice stretched with a child's grace to reach the pedals, her polished black shoes gently toeing the brass. She could not look at me. She waited for the sound of my opening chord to begin.

My piano had not improved. Mary Alice's had not improved, and Susan's had perhaps deteriorated. We would work in concert with our instruments to order the sounds and give what we had to the music. Over the seats and before the mingy floor-to-ceiling divider I could see in the maroon linoleum wet with tracked-in rain an oscillating image of Susan coming to love me, of our raising wondrous children in a sunroomed house, with a Steinway and their growing young arms displaying a heartening gift for the instrument.

Susan would be unaware of the gift the future held for her: her life as a stirring solo across the harmonic map by Fatha Hines. Her life performed with the left-handed abandon of Oscar Peterson. Her life joined in mine and mine finding meaning in hers, if only I would have — and I knew I did — if only I would have the patience to wait.

Runway

He often wondered, sitting at the window watching Billy and Theophilus play in the street, what he would do if one of them were hit by a car. Billy sat against the telephone pole, where he always did, near the end of the driveway, throwing a chewed-up tennis ball off the tire of a parked car. The ball perpetually fooled Theophilus with its change of direction. Depending on how Billy threw it the ball would ricochet or arc softly back, and the dog, sprinting at the first motion of his arm, was endlessly surprised by all trajectories. One ricochet caught the dog squarely in the forehead, and it wobbled comically and flopped over onto the pavement.

With a son like Billy you don't wonder things like that, Jay would find himself saying while shaving. He would peer at his image in the mirror.

And in the living room, nights, watching television with Billy on the floor in front of him, he'd think, Has the boy ever come close to doing anything reckless? Has the boy been anything less than all he should be?

He sat before the TV and clasped and unclasped the arms of his chair. He nudged his son with his foot.

"Quit it," Billy said.

"This is a good show," Jay said. "In case you didn't notice."

Billy made a small dismissive noise.

"By the way," Jay said. "Has anyone ever given you high praise? Anybody ever tell you you were the greatest?"

"You did," Billy said. "Yesterday."

Their eyes went back to the TV, and Jay drummed his fingers on his knee.

"Oh," Anne said, on the sofa. It was her terminal boredom voice. She had a film book, a big coffee table thing, on her lap. She'd gotten it on a good deal from a publisher's clearinghouse. He could see Garbo upside down, regarding them.

David Janssen was squinting at the street through some venetian blinds. Jay had lost the story for a second. What was he doing inside the house?

"So where do you go on these walks of yours?" Anne asked.

"I'm watching," Jay said.

"He won't tell you," Billy said.

Anne flipped a few more pages in her film book. She closed it with a thump.

There was a commercial and Jay stood up. He saw Anne looking at him and crossed to her and leaned over, his hands on his thighs, as if examining her face microscopically.

"You didn't answer my question," Anne finally said.

"You're very beautiful," Jay said. He said it as if after much debate as to how to put it.

"I know," Anne said. "I'm gorgeous. Where're you going?"

He kissed her, and held the kiss longer than she expected. Then he straightened up.

"Where are you *going*?" she said.

"You sound tired," he said.

"I *am* tired." She switched off the lamp and looked back at the television. She was eighteen in its light. "This is over. I'll turn it off."

"No, it's all right. I'll be back in a little while." He touched his wife's ear, for a goodbye, and slipped away.

Theophilus had almost been hit once, by an old Le Sabre. Jay heard the screech but no body sound and no horn, and he reacted he remembered later like he was underwater, swimming futilely toward the front door and the yard in time to see Anne already crouching over the dog, making sure it was all right, with another arm on Billy's shoulder. Billy was lifting and dropping Theo's front paw in a rudimentary medical exam and the driver was waiting for Jay to get there to exchange apologies before leaving. Jay hadn't had anything to say and the guy had gotten into his Le Sabre and waved like he'd enjoyed the visit. Anne had said on the way back to the house, What were you, asleep? and he hadn't been able to shake the feeling of being underwater until hours later, watching television.

Behind him Anne surfed channels in frustration with her remote, and Billy said, "Ma. Leave it on one." Jay eased past the dog asleep on the floor in the kitchen. He opened the door softly. The dog was immediately on its feet but too late to get to the door. It stood with its front paws on the windowsill, backlit by the kitchen light. Jay stretched in the driveway, rubbing his forearms against the chill. August and the nights were already cool. He left the dog panting silently behind the glass and crossed the yard to

FAMILY

the street, conjuring up Anne's face in the light of the television. He was away from the lights of his house quickly, and then he left the streetlights, off-white and quiet, behind him as well.

The lights receded and the darkness and quiet increased. His street was a dead end. He was heading for the fence on the grassy bluff beyond the pavement, and for the airport beyond the fence.

They had an arrangement for Thursday nights: he got to see his shows, Anne got to see hers, and Billy got to see his. The times lined up. They had a VCR but only used it for rental movies. On other nights when shows competed Jay sometimes stuck it out and sometimes didn't. When he didn't he sat by the window in the kitchen with the lights out. Anne would say to Billy, "Your father's in there communing with the darkness."

The Sieberts' dog, an Irish setter/beagle mix, barked at the rattle of the chain link every time Jay reached the fence, and kept barking until he slid underneath it and got down to the base of the bluffs. He tried not to let the dog hurry him, picking his way through the brambles and fallen birches in the moonlight. He was off his usual path—here was some splintered and ragged sumac, where he expected a small clearing—but it was no problem; he knew his way around.

Billy was nine and Theophilus was four and Anne was thirty-five, and Jay spent as much time as he could with them, watching. They were all happy. When he thought of his family he thought of the dog snuffing under the azalea, sprinting in bursts after squirrels and birds, barking and leaping splay legged at the tennis ball. Anne was happy. She loved her job and concentrated on it at home in a knit-browed, serious way that he admired; she loved her books, her cooking, her landscaping. Billy was happy. He had

168

his father and mother and Theo. Theo was happy. Everybody was happy.

As he expected, once on the bottom, at runway level, he had no problems. He headed for the four red threshold lights spanning diagonally away from him. He kept an eye out for security vehicles. He moved through the high ground cover the way he moved through his own darkened house. He found the huge chevrons of the overrun area, and then his feet were on the landing threshold, and the hard surface of the runway itself.

He stood between the central red lights. They seemed attentive, obedient and waiting. He crossed to one and held his hand over it, the red glowing up through his skin and between his fingers, creating a pleasing, instant X ray. He held on to the thick, warm glass and leaned back, squeezing, staring out into the darkness and stars in the direction of the approach pattern of the planes.

He pulled away from the lights, finally, moving toward the center of the runway, the circling beam of the tower in the distance calming him. He crossed the nonprecision approach markings, great, white parallel squares, and stood over the sweeping number of the runway designation. The number was 28. It was probably the compass bearing, as well. He sat down. He turned back to the four red lights, still silent and waiting. Then he lay back, spread-eagle, and looked up into the darkness.

It wasn't long before he heard the first plane. It was a light, far-off buzzing, starting out beyond his left arm and circling quietly, slowly, around him until it was coming, harder and louder, from below his heels. He told himself he wouldn't look, he'd keep his eyes straight up, but when it got so loud it seemed already on him he jerked his head up, his chin hitting his chest, and caught the landing lights full in the face. They passed over him in an instant, streaking up the runway far ahead of the plane, leaving him momentarily blinded, but everything reappeared immediately, and right overhead swinging toward him like a great pendulum were the red and white running lights, spread out unevenly in a line and gleaming on the smooth underside of the wings and fuselage, the wheels swaying low beneath them. He rolled, face pressed against the pavement, as the noise rushed over him in a wave, shaking him, and was gone.

He rose to his elbows and lay on his belly, watching the plane skirt into the darkness, the lights slowly joining the concentration of lights around the tower.

He marked the spot in his mind and computed how far into the runway the next spot should be. Then he left, heading for the bluff at a good speed, because the airport security wasn't that bad.

There was no pattern to the runway visits. He varied their frequency to baffle airport security. He was certainly reported each time by the incoming pilot. Sometimes he waited as much as three months to go out, watching the security jeeps on their rounds through the chain-link fence at the end of the street. Sometimes he went as often as once a week. This week he was going twice: Thursday and Saturday.

Saturday night he heard a twin-engine, it sounded like, even before he'd found his spot. He went to his knees and scuttled forward, approximating, and turned around. The lights were banking, slowly coming around to level, parallel now to the threshold lights beyond the runway's edge. The noise increased, and he picked up the landing lights slipping slowly along the ground, suddenly speeding up and flashing over him as the roar grew louder and the lights sank closer, and at the last moment he flattened out as much as he could on the surface of the tarmac, turning his face as his ears filled with sound and his clothing shook and he felt it touch down hard behind him, the shock traveling through him, and he knew, as he got up, running for the bluff, that the next time, farther out onto the runway, might be the last time.

He remembered a movie he'd seen some years ago called *The Magnificent Seven*. In it, Steve McQueen, one of a group of gunfighters who have banded together for no apparent reason to protect a poor Mexican town from bandits, is asked by the bandit chief why they stay and fight against insurmountable odds for no reward. He replies, "Well, it's like a guy I once knew in Waco. Took off all his clothes one day and jumped into a cactus. I asked him why he did it."

And the bandit chief says impatiently, "Well? What did he say?"

And McQueen replies, "He said it seemed like a good idea at the time."

When he got back Billy and Theo were in the sunroom, Theo still nose to the window. Had the dog been like that the whole time? Billy was sitting in the lawn chair they kept inside and was shelling peanuts on his lap. Billy said, "So where'd you go, Dad?"

He realized he was still wired and flushed and he put his hand over the top of Billy's head and mussed his hair, though he never did that. He said, "I went for a walk. What're you, a cop?"

But Billy held his ground, staring up at him, and he was forced to turn to Anne, who came around the corner from the kitchen, the phone to her ear and the cord stretched taut. She nodded hello and said, "Mother. He just came in."

She gave him a stern look and he kissed her until she had to pull away to say, "Yes, Mother, yes, I'm listening."

"Mr. Mystery," Billy said behind him. Jay crossed the kitchen, ducking while Anne held the cord up, and dropped onto the sofa in the living room, casting around for the remote. Billy had left it turned around atop the TV, the electric eye facing him.

Sometimes he thought, You're a responsible young man, you need to consider this, but nothing coherent or plausible came to him when he did. Nothing made him do it, he realized, mowing the first summer grass or piling clippings into the trunk to take to the dump. Part of the reason, he knew, was the way it felt that first split second when he heard a Cessna or an Allegheny or something make that distant turn, start that faint buzz way off in the night.

He'd been out nine times. He was six-one and each time he went out he moved six feet and an inch farther down the runway, each time coming closer to the touchdown point of most aircraft. Of course, there'd always been the chance that someone would touch down early, as well.

He bustled around the house after supper for a week, cleaning, fixing, storing, and straightening, and Anne watched him happily and took him aside and said, smiling, "You're a real dynamo this week, know it?" When he started to pull away, hedge clippers in hand, she got serious and added, "You're wonderful, you know that?"

He settled his affairs at work, getting the last shipments of the week out two days early and working with such efficiency even for him that his fellow workers were sure something was up. He made sure before he left on Friday that someone could cover for him Monday if he was late or couldn't make it.

The guys at Sikorsky knew he was a good worker. And they knew he was crazy.

He wasn't inclined to believe them.

He didn't feel wild or out of control when he did the things he did.

When he was five every Sunday night for a week he jumped off the roof of the porch of the old house on Spruce Street. He was practicing landing and rolling.

When he was seventeen he and a friend raced twin Kawasakis off a dock and into the Housatonic River. The Kawasakis had taken two weeks to clean and get back into shape. When he was twenty-five, ten years ago, he climbed the roof of the main hangar at Sikorsky on his lunch break. It was his first year on the job.

Two years after that he'd found himself on his belly behind the forklift in Hangar 6, out of reach of the light drizzle slicking the helicopter pad, thirty-three yards away from him, and the HH-52 warming up on it.

He'd measured the thirty-three yards. He'd measured everything, including the time it would take to cross them and the time from the first revving of its turbines that it would take the HH-52 to get airborne and out of reach. He'd figured out the best day (Saturday), the best weather conditions (rainy), and the best copter (the 52, with its massive pods surrounding the landing gear) for what he planned. The landing gear would be his handholds, and the pods would shield him initially from the tower's view.

The turbines went into their high metallic rush and the blades of the big ship pitched and he counted one, two, three, and broke for the copter, spattering across the gleaming blacktop and into the rotor wash, approaching from the rear diagonally to avoid pilot detection and the tail rotor, and he jumped as the landing gear was lifting up and swaying away from him. He caught one arm around the inside strut and pulled himself up and around, banging his head on the undercarriage. There was no hesitation in the climb so he knew he was okay, and the copter immediately banked out over the Housatonic, and with his head throbbing he swung his legs down, looking past them to the water spinning away below, and then let go, the noise of the rotors filling his ears all the way down.

Somewhere along the line he decided to go back to the runway Sunday night. He asked Anne if she wanted to go out to dinner Saturday. Get a sitter for Billy. She loved the idea. When she left the bathroom Saturday night, ready to go, he thought her beauty must increase in some way proportionate to her happiness.

He'd first thought of the runway on a Christmas Day. It came to him as a visual image while he was stuffing scattered wrapping paper into a brown grocery bag. Billy was confusing Theo with an orange Nerf basketball by compressing it and hiding it in his fist. Anne was on the phone, in her blue nightgown with the tiny embroidery on the shoulders. He got up, got dressed, kissed her on the cheek, and headed out into the snow. It was very cold. It occurred to him before he reached the airport that they wouldn't have had time to plow yet, but he kept going. Out over the runway the snow had drifted into little ridges that reminded him of the roof of a dog's mouth. There was a bright glare over everything from the morning light. He crossed to where he judged the center of the runway must be, and lay down, sinking and looking up at the sky.

Sunday morning he bought the papers. He played catch with Billy down the length of the driveway, enjoying the feel of the old Rawlings. He threw Billy grounders, soft line drives, pop-ups.

He had drinks in the backyard with Anne. He helped her with

the pork chops for supper. He helped Billy with his homework.

When that was over they joined Anne in the den. She was catching the end of *Moby Dick*. Gregory Peck was nailing a gold coin to the masthead and making speeches.

Anne looked over at him and gave him a smile. He was starting to get fidgety. He said he was going to take a look around. He poured some cranberry juice from the refrigerator and drank it. He washed out the glass in the sink. He took Theo out to let him take a leak, jingling change in his pockets while the dog decided on a bush. Then he let it back in, closed the door behind it, and went down the driveway, enjoying the summer smells and heading down the street at a jog.

Anne never found out about the copter ride, though it had been in the papers (a UPI photographer there to cover another test flight had happened to get a shot of him on the way down, a tiny figure, grainy and blurred; it had caused a minor sensation at Sikorsky security). She knew about other things, including the hangar roof, and when he did things like that she told him she wanted to understand. She also asked if he ever thought about her and Billy. Things like that she expected more from the kind of kids she hoped to keep Billy away from.

He didn't answer because he loved her and wanted to protect her, and also because he didn't know how to explain it without sounding as if he were refusing to explain it.

He took his time on the bluffs. The Sieberts' dog kicked up a racket. He imagined he heard another dog answering. He ran his fingers over the chain link of the fence before slipping under it, sliding through the damp smooth hole scuffed in the dirt. Halfway down he stopped and surveyed the runway. Then he leaned out over the slope and cantered down, every step sure, digging his heels in the gravel and slaloming around the bushes and larger stones.

At the bottom he heard the rumble of something big, and a four-engine Allegheny came thundering over the bluffs to his right, close enough that he could see heads in the windows. It swept over the runway, its rear wheels slamming down with a tremendous, murderous screech, right, he estimated as he hurried toward the overrun area in its wake, where he would momentarily be lying.

He stopped at the markings and crouched, looking for security activity, and then crossed to the middle. He found his old mark, measured out from it, and set his new one. He lay back on his elbows, made one last check of the runway around him, and settled in, looking up at the stars. Something rustled in the high grass. He waited.

Far off he could hear cars moving, beyond the tower on the other side of the airport. From that grew another sound.

He looked back for the tower and caught in the gleam of one of its circling beams a Pilgrim Airlines twin-engine banking slowly around toward his strip.

He lay back, trying to keep still, the plane circling gradually in the darkness off to the left, disappearing beyond the bluff as it made its final gliding bank into its approach, its engines still audible. He could feel them getting higher in pitch. He watched the section of bluff visible over his feet, waiting for the red and white lights to explode over it toward him, but felt vibration coming from the opposite direction as well, and twisted around and there were the headlights of the security jeep down by the tower, bouncing along the shoulder of the runway. He got up in a crouch but then hesitated, and turned to face the bluff, the Pilgrim's engines roaring behind it now, and lay back down.

Then he saw Theo.

He picked up movement in his peripheral vision and turned as the dog reached the runway. He shouted something as Billy piled out of the darkness onto the tarmac, too, slipping to his knees. He shot a look back at the jeep while trying to push the dog away, and Billy was shouting something and running toward them, and then the dog cringed and there was a roar as the Pilgrim twin-engine burst over the bluffs. Billy froze looking up at the huge lighted dark shape swinging down toward him, screaming, maybe; Jay couldn't hear. He grabbed Theo by the skin and hair of his neck and dove at Billy, throwing the dog as far as he could, sending him sprawling and skidding off the runway, and hitting Billy in the midsection and driving him hard onto his back as the twin-engine hit beside them, the wing sweeping over, and was gone.

Billy was crying and twisting around in his arms as the jeep pulled up alongside, becoming audible only as the plane taxied farther down the runway. Men in blue vinyl jackets grabbed them. One was chasing Theo around the scrub nearby. Even then and there they were asking questions, which he waved off, trying to indicate he'd answer everything soon. His voice was coming back to him with his hearing. Someone shook him, and he nodded, yes. He was watching Theo, who was all right. He was concentrating on Anne, and on not letting go of Billy.

Krakatau

I was twelve years old when I figured out that the look my brother would get around his eyes probably meant that there was a physiological basis for what was wrong with him. Six years later as a college freshman I was flipping through Gardner's *Art Through the Ages*, fifth edition, and was shocked to come across that same look, Donnie's eyes, peering out at me from Géricault's *Madwoman*. The madwoman in question was elderly, wrapped in some kind of cloak. She wore a white bonnet. Her eyes looked away from the painter as if just piecing together the outlines of another conspiracy. She'd outsmarted the world, and was going to outsmart this painter. I recognized the hatred, the sheer animosity for *everything*, unconcealed. Red lines rimmed her eyelids in a way that did not resemble eyestrain or fatigue. It was as if the mind behind the eyes was soaking in anguish. The next morning my Intro to Art History professor flashed a slide of the painting, ten feet wide, on the screen in front of us. A gum-chewing class went silent. "How'd you like to wake up to that in the morning?" the professor joked.

That night I called my father. He and my mother and Donnie still lived in the house Donnie and I grew up in, two hours away. I was in the little public phone booth in the dorm. It was lined with cork and the cork was scribbled over with phone numbers and ballpoint drawings of dicks.

Donnie answered. "How ya doin'," he said.

"I'm all right," I said. "How about you?"

He snorted.

Some kid opened the door to the booth like I wasn't in there and poked his head in. "Who *you* talkin' to?" he said.

"No one," I said. "Get outta here."

The kid made a face and shut me back in.

"Who was that?" Donnie asked.

"Some asshole," I said. I didn't say anything else. Donnie sniffed in like he was doing a line of something.

"You wanna talk to Daddy?" he said. He was four years older but he still used words like that.

"Yeah, put him on," I said. You couldn't talk to him for five minutes? I thought to myself.

He put his hand over the receiver. Things went on on the other end, muffled. "Hey there," my father finally said.

"Hey," I said back. There was some dead air.

"What's up?" my father said.

"Not much," I said. I'd planned on my father being alone. I don't know why. My brother never went out. "Just callin'."

I was rubbing my knuckles hard over the cork next to the phone's coin box. Pieces were scrolling off as if from an eraser. "How's the money holding out?" my father said. Donnie made a comment behind him.

"Is he standing right next to you?" I asked.

"Yeah. Why?" my father said, instantly more alert. When I was little and I wanted his attention I just mentioned a problem with Donnie. By college it had gotten to the point that hashing over worries about my brother was pretty much it in terms of contact with my parents.

"I wanted to ask you something," I said.

"Is there something I should know about?" he said. Donnie was always doing things that we kept from him because he got so upset.

"Nothin' big. Maybe I should call back," I said.

"Awright. I'll see you," he said. It was a code we'd worked before.

"Short call," I heard Donnie say before my father hung up.

When my father called back, we went over the physiological thing again. I'd run this by him before. We thought drug therapy might be a possible way out.

I could see the blowups coming in Donnie's eyes. I could see the redness. And I usually didn't stop whatever I was doing to help them come on.

The problem was that Donnie had had drug therapy, back in the Dawn of Time, in 1969. Who knew anything? Various combinations of doctors tried various combinations of drugs. Most of the drugs had humiliating side effects. My brother became a master at lying to the doctors about what he'd taken and what he'd squirreled away, further confusing the issue. He came out eight months later as one of the Yale–New Haven Institute's complete failures—"We throw up our hands with him," the resident told my parents—and with a loathing even for Bufferin.

. . .

"In Géricault's paintings, suffering and death, battle frenzy, and madness amount to nature itself, for nature in the end is formless and destructive."

But really: how helpful are we going to find art history prose as an interpretive model?

We called the police six times on him. After high school I was home only a few weeks a year—the World Traveler, my father called me, caustically—yet I'd been home four of the six times we had to call the police. My father mentioned the coincidence.

While my brother was in a holding pen in New Orleans I received my B.S. from Swarthmore in geological engineering. While he was touring youth hostels on the East Coast on my father's dole, keeping to himself, a dour man in his late twenties surrounded by happy groups of much younger Europeans, I was getting my Ph.D. in geology from Johns Hopkins. He had a scramble of fine black hair that he almost never combed. He wore pastel polyester tank tops long after even Kmart shoppers had abandoned them. He had a little gut which he accentuated by tucking in his shirts and wearing too-tight pants without belts. While he was giving night school a shot in Florida I was mapping the geology of Mount Rainier. The fall he spent going through his old things at my parents' house and getting his baseball card collection sorted out, I spent crawling around ancient volcanoes in equatorial East Africa. The third time my parents had to call the police on him I was in a little boat in the Sunda Strait, getting my first look at Krakatau.

What were my parents supposed to do? They never went to college, and just wanted their sons comfortable and reasonably happy. A steady job in a stable business would have been nice. Instead one son disappeared into the academic ionosphere: I had to literally write down *postdoctoral fellow* so my mother could pull it out of her wallet and say it for people. She asked me to. They had a copy of *Volcanoes of the World* around the house, with my name listed among the fourteen junior authors contributing. My mother would say, "Here's his book." And their older son dropped out of high school because, as he put it, he was "being stared at." If I was hard to explain, my brother was impossible to explain. For relatives the etiquette was to ask about the younger one and then move on to the older one. I was never around and always doing well. He was always around and never doing well. Yes, doctors had seen him, and yes, he was clearly disturbed, but no one had a diagnosis, and as far as their ability to present him as a coherent story went, he operated in that maddening middle ground: too disturbed to function and not disturbed enough to be put away.

The first time we called the police because he threw me down the stairs. I was twelve, and he'd dropped out of high school the month before. We'd been arguing about sports, matching feats of memory by reciting NFL championship scores ("1963, fourteen–ten; 1964, twenty-seven–zero; 1965, twenty-three–thirteen"), and he'd heard the contempt in my voice. He'd been livid and my father's mediation attempts had consisted of stepping between us and shouting for my brother to go upstairs. He had, finally, shouting abuse the whole time about my privileged and protected status, and for once I thought I wasn't going to back down and went up after him, as homicidal as he was. At the top of the stairs I jabbed a finger in his chest. Shouting was going on. I watched his face move into some new area of energy. He lifted me up. My feet kicked above the risers like a toddler's, and then he threw me. I caught the banister with my hands and landed on my elbow and side. The stairs were carpeted. I got up, unhurt. "Play with pain," he shouted down the stairs at me. "Play with pain."

"You're gonna kill them both," I screamed up at him, pulling out the ultimate weapon, his guilt. I said it so they could hear. "They're gonna kill *me*," he screamed back.

My mother, father, and I sat around the kitchen table after the police had taken him away. The policeman had been awkward and embarrassed and stood around Donnie's room while Donnie packed a little blue duffel in silence. We could hear the creaks in the floorboards above us as the policeman shifted his weight from foot to foot. The routine was that the police would drive him to the bus station and tell him he couldn't come back for a while. Then the police would come back and talk to us. While we waited for that, my mother would outline the fatal mistakes my father had made raising my brother.

We were three co-conspirators each operating with a different plan. My mother's theory was that special treatment was his undoing. My father's theory was that explosions could be avoided if everyone did their utmost to work around him. My theory was that something cyclical and inexorable was going on, and that one way or another, sooner or later, he had to go off.

That night my father had taken as much abuse as he was able to. He shouted at both of us, "You can't treat him like a normal human being; you can't keep baiting him." He said, "It's like having a dog on a chain. You don't keep sticking fingers in his mouth." Then he said to me, "And your situation doesn't help."

What my father meant was that just by being alive I made my brother's life harder. In Donnie's eyes I was proof that whatever had happened to him—genetically, environmentally, whatever—hadn't been inevitable. One of his consolations had always been that something in the alchemy of the parenting he'd gotten had been so lethal that he had had to turn out the way he did. But I was the problem with that theory, because if that was true, then why wasn't the kid (he called me the kid) affected?

Whatever I achieved threw the mess he'd made of his life into sharper relief. He went to Catholic school and it ruined him; I went to Catholic school and got good grades. He was always shy and turned out to need hospitalization; I was always shy and turned out to be bookish.

At one point in Pompano Beach, he took a job as a dishwasher at a Bob's Big Boy. My mother's first response when she heard was to congratulate him. Her second was to remark that she thought they had machines for that now. That same day he went into work and the day manager was chatting him up. The day manager asked if he had any brothers or sisters. The day manager asked what his brother did. "He's a rocket scientist," Donnie said, up to his elbows in suds, thirty-eight years old.

My thesis adviser at Johns Hopkins always ate Fudgsicles while he looked over my work. All the charts and text he handled turned up with chocolate thumbprints. Slurping away, flipping through the data, he liked to ask, "What is it with you and Krakatoa, anyway?" He meant why was I so driven. He intentionally pronounced it the wrong way. He liked to think of himself as puckish.

The founder of the Smithsonian, James Smithson, explained his institute's interest in the subject this way: "A high interest attaches itself to volcanoes, and their ejections. They cease to be local phenomena; they become principal elements in the history of our globe; they connect its present with its former condition; and we have good grounds for supposing that in their flames are to be read its future destinies."

I quoted Smithson to my adviser as an answer. He shrugged and took out his Fudgsicle and said, "You can talk to someone like me now or talk to a shrink later."

Pictures came into my head periodically of what my brother must have gone through, on the road. He told me, occasionally, as well. When he traveled the country he stayed at youth hostels because they were so much cheaper, but he paid a price for it: he was pathological about his privacy, and there he had none. In Maine an older woman asked him about his hair. It was falling out. At Gettysburg some teenaged Germans took him out, got him drunk, and asked if he was attracted to one of the prettier girls in the group. Assuming that some sort of positive sexual fantasy was finally about to happen to him, he said yes, at which point they all laughed. He said he woke up the next morning near the site of Pickett's charge. A middle-aged couple with a video camera stood nearby, filming him alongside the stone wall.

The last time I was home he was on the road. We'd timed it that way. I spent one late night going through a family album that my mother was putting together in a spasm of masochism and love. Looking back over pictures of my brother developing year by year, his expressions progressively more closed off and miserable, brought back to me powerfully the first time I saw the sequence of photos tracking the birth of Paricutin, the Mexican volcano that grew from a tiny vent cone in a farmer's field.

The postdoctoral fellowship involved part-time work for SEAN, the Scientific Event Alert Network, which was designed to keep the geological and geophysical communities in touch about active volcanoes throughout the world. I compiled and cross-referenced known data about older eruptions so that it could be manipulated for studies of recent and expected volcanism. Which was where all my work on Krakatau came in.

My thesis adviser had been the first to point out that I'd developed what people in the field call a bias. I had a heightened appreciation for the value of eyewitness accounts. I always leaned toward the Catastrophists' viewpoint that while the ordinary eruptions needed to be documented, the complete cataclysms had the real answers; they were the ones that had to be milked for all they could yield. "What do we have here?" my adviser would say wearily as he picked up another new batch of text. "More screamers?" "Screamer" was his term for Krakatau eyewitnesses. He called their rough calculations, made under what geologists would laconically call stressful situations, "Fay Wray calculations."

And yet, often enough for me, working backward from a dispassionate scientific measurement—the tidal gauges at Jakarta, say—I'd be able to corroborate one more eyewitness account.

In my dumpy carrel at the Grad Library I had narrowed the actual subject of my thesis down to the precise causes of the Krakatau tsunamis that swamped Java and Sumatra. This was a reasonably controversial topic. There were all sorts of wave-forming mechanisms, all of which could have operated to some extent at Krakatau. The problem was to understand which mechanism was the dominant one. The expectation was not so much that I would find a solution to the problem as add something intelligent to the debate.

The first two years I worked eighteen-plus hours a day. I never got home, almost never talked to my family. Crises came and went; what did I care? I combed everything: the Library of Congress, the National Archives, the U.S. Geological Survey, the Smithsonian Library, the British Museum, the Royal Society of London, the Royal Institute for the Tropics, the Volcanological Survey of Indonesia, the *Bulletin Volcanologique*. I needed more help than anyone else on earth. And I turned out to possess the height of scientific naïveté. I believed everyone I read. Everyone sounded so reasonable. Everyone's figures looked so unassailable. I was a straw in the wind. I labored through Verbeek's original monograph from 1885 as well as later papers by Wharton, Yokoyama, and Latter. At one point my adviser told me with exasperation, "Hey, know what? It's not likely that everyone's right." I incorporated this into my text. I wrote, "Nevertheless, it is safe to assume that all of these contradictory theories cannot be accurate."

I uncovered a few things. I turned up a few photographs of the devastation from as early as 1886. I tracked down some math errors in the computations of the air waves. Then, in 1983, the centennial year of the eruption, everything I'd done was surpassed, the dugout canoe swamped by the *Queen Mary*: the Smithsonian published *Krakatau 1883: The Volcanic Eruption and Its Effects*, providing me with 456 phone-book-sized pages to pore over. It would have been my fantasy book, if I hadn't already sunk two years into a thesis.

Everything had to be retooled. My new topic became this baggy, reactive thing that just got me through, something along the lines of This Big New Book: Is It Almost Completely the Last Word? The answer was yes.

I had a Career Crisis. My personal hygiene suffered. I stared openmouthed out windows. I sat around inert most mornings, working my way through tepid coffee and caramels for breakfast.

I faced for the first time the stunning possibility that everything I touched was not going to turn to gold.

My mother called to see how I was doing. I put on a brave front. She called back the next day and said, "I told your brother you weren't doing so well."

"What'd he say?" I asked.

"Nothing," she said.

"I'm worried I'm gonna end up like him," I joked.

We heard a click on the line. "Uh-oh," my mother said.

A week later my brother sent me *Krakatoa, East of Java*. He'd taped it off a Disaster Film Festival and mailed it in a box wrapped in all directions with duct tape. Maximilian Schell, Rossano Brazzi, Brian Keith: that kind of movie. What my brother remembered was that the second half of the film—the eruption itself, and the tidal waves that followed—was the really unendurable part, and always had been for me, ever since I sat through its sorry cheesiness with him when I was thirteen years old.

He didn't include a note with it, and he didn't have to: it was exactly his sense of humor, with the aggression directed everywhere at once.

Even my brother, in other words, had seen through the schematic of my private metaphor and knew the answer to my adviser's question: Why is he obsessed with volcanoes? Because they go off, regardless of what anyone can do. And because, when they do go off, it's no one's fault. Volcanology: the science of standing around and cataloging the devastation.

My father discouraged my brother from visiting me, wherever I was. He did it for my benefit, and my brother's. He was the Peacemaker, he thought; if he wasn't around, anything could happen.

My brother didn't particularly enjoy visiting me—anything new in my life seemed to cause him to take stock of his—but he had few places to go. Occasionally he'd call, with my father in the room, and drop a hint. My father would hear the hint and intervene in the background. The excuse he always came up with—I was too busy, I had all this work, this was a bad time for me to be receiving visitors—could not have helped my brother. But if he wanted to keep us apart, what else could he say? My brother was too busy?

"This isn't the greatest time anyway," I'd say. "What about around Thanksgiving? What're you doing around Thanksgiving?"

Knowing full well that the tiniest lack of enthusiasm would destroy whatever chance there was that he'd work up the courage to visit.

Donnie was sixteen when we went through family counseling. He'd been out of high school two months, and had had three jobs: landscaping, freight handling for UPS, and working construction. The construction work was for an uncle who owned a company. We'd had our first incident involving the police. That was how my father referred to it. I was twelve. I had relatively little to do during the sessions. I conceived of the time as an opportunity to prove to this psychiatrist that it wasn't all my parents' fault, what had happened. I acted normal.

Donnie called my father the Mediator. The shrink asked what he meant by that. Donnie said, "Mediator. You know. Zookeeper. What the fuck." It was the "What the fuck" that broke my heart.

Even then I had a mouth on me, as my mother would say. Christmas Eve we watched the Roddy McDowall/David Hartman version of *Miracle on 34th Street,* a version my brother hadn't seen but insisted was the best one. It was on for four minutes before it was clear to everyone in the room that it was terrible. Which made my brother all the more adamant in his position. The holidays were hard on him. We'd given up on the family counseling a few weeks before, as if to get ready for Christmas.

In the movie Sebastian Cabot did a lot of eye-twinkle stuff, whatever the situation. I made relentless fun of it. I mimicked Cabot's accent and asked if Santa came from England, stuff like that. I was rolling. Even my father was snickering. Roddy McDowall launched into something on the Spirit of Christmas and I said it sounded like he was more interested in getting to know some of the elves. Donnie took the footstool in front of him and smashed the TV tube. That was the second time we had to call the police.

They took him to the Bridgeport bus station, 8:30 at night on Christmas Eve. The two cops who came to the house wanted to leave him with us, but he wouldn't calm down. One cop told him, "If you don't lighten up we're gonna have to get you out of here and *keep* you out of here," so Donnie started in on what he was going to do to each one of us as soon as the cop took off: "First I'm gonna break *his* fucking neck, and then *her* fucking neck, and then *his* fucking neck." Stuff like that. It was raining, and when they led him out, he had on a New York Jets windbreaker and no hat.

My father drove down to the bus station a half hour later to see if he was still there. The roads were frozen and it took him an hour to get back. My mother vacuumed up the glass from the picture tube. Then she sat in her bedroom with the little TV, flipping back and forth from A *Christmas Carol* to the Mass at St. Peter's.

When my father got back he made some tea and wandered the house. I remembered the nuns talking about the capacities of

Christ's love and thought, What kind of reptile *are* you? I was filled with wonder at myself.

I finally went to midnight Mass, alone. My mother just waved me off when I asked if she wanted to go. I found myself once I got there running through a fractured Catechism, over and over: — Who loves us? —We love us. —Who does this to us? —We do this to ourselves. —Whose victims are we? —We are our own victims.

The next morning I was supposed to come downstairs and open presents.

Around noon we gathered in front of the tree with our coffee. I suppose we were hoping Donnie was going to come back. I opened the smallest present in my pile, a Minnesota Viking coffee mug, and said, "That's great, thanks," and my parents' faces were so desolate that we quit right there.

He called from the bus station on the twenty-seventh. He opened one or two of his presents a week after that. The rest stayed where they were even after the tree came down. Some of them my mother gave the next year to our cousins. We never put tags on our presents; we just told each other who they belonged to.

The third time they had to call the police I was fourteen thousand miles away, fulfilling my dream, standing on what was left of Krakatau. I brought back pieces of pumice for everybody. Donnie had called my mother's sisters whores, and she'd slapped him, and he'd knocked her to the kitchen floor. When he was going full tilt he tried everything verbally until something clicked. He was thirty-four then and she was sixty. My father left his eggs frying at the stove and started wrestling with him. He was sixty-three. My brother let him wrestle.

Krakatau

. . .

From page five of my thesis: "Early theories explaining the size of the Krakatau explosion held that millions of tons of rock had unfortunately formed a kind of plug, so that pressure-relieving venting was not allowed, making the final detonations all the more cataclysmic. But in fact the opposite might also have been true: gas fluxing of the conduits and the release of pressure through massive cracks may have hastened the catastrophe, since once the vents were opened, the eruption might have grown, as deeper and hotter layers of magma were tapped, leading to the exhaustion of the reservoir, and following that, the collapse of its roof."

My adviser had written in the margin: "Anything new here?"

I had three reasons for my own passivity: selfishness, cowardice, and resentment.

As Donnie got older the anger inside him was not decreasing but increasing. His rage was driven by humiliation, and year by year he felt his situation—forty-one and living at home, unemployed, forty-two and living at home, unemployed—to be more and more humiliating. The friends-and-family question So what are you up to?—fraught when he was eighteen—was when he was forty suffused with subtextual insult. His violence was more serious. His threats were more pointed. He defined himself more and more as a misfit, and more and more he seemed to think that the gesture that was going to be necessary to redeem such a life, with each passing day, needed to be grander, more radical.

He was forty-two. I was thirty-eight, two hours away, mostly out of contact, and all of my failures with him were focused in one weekend that summer, when, despite everything, he visited. We spent two days circling each other, watching sports and old movies and making fun of what we saw. His last night there he told me about some of his fantasies. One of them ended with, "They'd *think* they knew what happened, but how could they *prove* it? How could they *prove* anything?" My stomach dropped out.

It was late. I'd turned off the TV. I could see his eyes in the dark. "Listen," I said. "You've gotta see somebody." "Don't you think I know that?" he said.

After two late movies he fell asleep facedown on the sofa. I went to my office and called Psychological Services at the university. The guy on call gave me a referral number.

"I don't think you understand," I told him. "This isn't a kind of wait-and-see situation."

"Are you saying he should be picked up, for his own good?" the guy said. There was a buzzing on the line while he waited for my answer.

"No," I said.

The next morning my brother was leaving. I stood by my parents' car while he settled into the driver's seat. I told him I had the name of a guy he should talk to. "Thanks," he said.

"You want the name?" I said.

"Sure," he said. I could see his eyes, see a blowup coming on again. This was excruciating for him.

I fumbled around in my pockets. "I don't have a pencil," I said. "You gonna remember?"

"Sure," he said. I told him the name. He nodded, put the car in gear, said goodbye, and backed out of the driveway.

I warned my parents. Which, I thought to myself, would help my conscience later.

. . .

Why didn't I help? Why did I stand aside, peering down the rails toward the future site of the train wreck? Because even if he didn't know it, all along, he was the lucky one. Because he was the black sheep, he was the squeaky wheel, he was the engine that generated love from my parents.

I kept hoping that my worst feelings had been left behind in childhood, and that only analysis, diagnosis, remained.

Volcanoes, volcanoes, volcanoes. In a crucial way he didn't resemble volcanoes at all. Most volcanoes look like oceans. Because they're *under* oceans. Nothing happening for hundreds of years. Something destructive surfacing only very very rarely: who did that *really* sound like?

The first record of explosions came months early, May 20 at 10:55 a.m., when the director of the Observatory at Batavia, now Jakarta, noticed vibrations and the banging of loose windows in his house. Explosions brought lighter articles down from the shelves at Anjer. There was this homey little description from the captain of the German warship *Elisabeth*, in the Sunda Strait: "We saw from the island a white cumulus cloud rising fast. After half an hour, it reached a height of 11,000 m. and started to spread, like an umbrella." Or this, from the same ship's Marine chaplain, now seventeen nautical miles away: "It was convoluted like a giant coral stock, resembling a club or cauliflower head, except that everything was in imposing gigantic internal motion, driven by enormous pressure from beneath. Slowly it became clear that the top of the entire continuously growing phenomenon was beginning to lean towards us."

Or this, from a telegraph master on the Java Coast: "I remained at the office the whole morning and then went for a meal, intending to return at two. I met another man near the beach, and we remained there for a few minutes. Krakatau was already in eruption, and we plainly heard the rumbling in the distance. I observed an alternate rising and falling of the sea, and asked my companion whether the tide was ebbing or flowing. He remarked that it seemed to be getting unusually dark."

Or this, from the captain of the Irish steamer *Charles Bal:* "At 2:30 we noticed some agitation about the point of Krakatau, clouds or something being propelled from the NE point with great velocity. At 3:00 we heard all around and above us the sounds of a mighty artillery barrage, getting evermore furious and alarming; and the matter, whatever it was, was being propelled with even more velocity to the NE. It looked like a blinding rain, a furious moiling squall. By 4:00 the explosions had joined to form a continuous roar, and darkness had spread across the sky."

And here's what I imagine, from the eyewitnesses who spent those last minutes standing around with their hands in their pockets on the Java Coast and Sumatra, from Lampong Bay to Sebesi and all the other islands in the strait:

Some made out an enormous wave in the distance like a mountain rushing onwards, followed by others that seemed greater still.

Some made out a dark black object rising through the gloom, traveling towards the shore like a low range of hills, but they knew there were no hills in that part of the strait.

Some made out a dark line swelling the curve of the horizon, thickening as they watched.

Some heard the roar of the first wave, and the cry "A flood is coming."

Some heard the rushing wind driven before the immense dark wall.

Some heard a whipsawing noise and saw the great black thing a long way off, a cliff of water, trees and houses disappearing beneath it. They felt it through the earth as they ran for sloping ground. They made for the steepest ravines. There was a great crush. Those below climbed the backs of those above. The marks where this took place are still visible. Some of those who washed off must have dragged others down with them. Some must have felt those above giving way, and let go.

But this is the only account hand-copied and tacked to my bulletin board, the testimony of a Dutch pilot caught on shore near Anjer, a city now gone: "The moment of greatest anguish was not the actual destruction of the wave. The worst part by far was afterwards, when I knew I was saved, and the receding flood carried back past me the bodies of friends and neighbors and family. And I remembered clawing past other arms and legs as you might fight through a bramble. And I thought, 'The world is our relentless adversary, rarely outwitted, never tiring.' And I thought, 'I would give all these people's lives, once more, to see something so beautiful again.'"

A NOTE ON THE TYPE

The text of this book was set in Electra, a typeface designed by W. A. Dwiggins (1880–1956). This face cannot be classified as either modern or old style. It is not based on any historical model, nor does it echo any particular period or style. It avoids the extreme contrasts between thick and thin elements that mark most modern faces, and it attempts to give a feeling of fluidity, power, and speed.

Composed by NK Graphics,
Keene, New Hampshire
Printed and bound by
The Haddon Craftsmen,
Scranton, Pennsylvania
Designed by Virginia Tan